4/22

The
Frightened
Bride

Barbara Cartland

THE FRIGHTENED BRIDE
A Bantam Book / May 1975
2nd printing
3rd printing
4th printing
5th printing

All rights reserved.
Copyright © 1975 by Barbara Cartland
This book may not be reproduced in whole or in part, by
mimeograph or any other means, without permission.
For information address: Bantam Books, Inc.

Published simultaneously in the United States and Canada

Bantam Books are published by Bantam Books, Inc. Its trade-
mark, consisting of the words "Bantam Books" and the por-
trayal of a bantam, is registered in the United States Patent
Office and in other countries. Marca Registrada. Bantam
Books, Inc., 666 Fifth Avenue, New York, New York 10019.

PRINTED IN THE UNITED STATES OF AMERICA

Author's Note

I visited Udaipur—the City of Dreams—for the first time in 1974. It is without exception the most beautiful, the most ethereal, romantic place I have ever seen. The Lake Palace is now a hotel, but its marble walls, pinnacles of amber and jade, its flowers, orange and lemon trees are still brilliant against the mosiacs.

The present Maharana—the 'Sun of the Hindus'—handsome and charming, gave me the classic history of Rajasthan written by Lt. Colonel James Todd, political agent to the Western Rajput States, and published in 1835. To these books I owe the background of Udaipur in this novel.

The description of Bombay and the glories of Parell are all authentic. Now Raj Bhavan—the Governor's residence is an unassuming cluster of bungalows at Malabar Point. Parell was abandoned after a Governor's wife died there of cholera.

Then after Bombay had suffered a fearful visitation of plague in 1896—believed by some of the more loyal Indians to have been a Divine punishment for the besmearing of Queen Victoria's Statue—the house was turned into a plague research laboratory, which it remains to this day.

Chapter One

1886

"No!" the Duke of Uxbridge said firmly.

In the pale winter light coming through the windows of his London house he looked very old, wizened and almost gnome-like.

"Please listen to me before you decide," the man sitting opposite him begged.

The contrast between the two men was startling.

Major Kelvin Ward had been spoken of as the smartest man in the British Army, and just to look at him in ordinary clothes was to realise that his clear-cut features and broad shoulders would be enhanced by regimentals.

"If it gives you any satisfaction, I am prepared to hear what you have to say," the Duke replied. "But my answer will be the same."

"I want you to realise my position, Sir," Kelvin Ward said. "You know that my mother's long

1

illness and her surgical operations cost over five thousand pounds and that I had to go to the Money Lenders for the money."

"You can hardly expect me to feel it was my responsibility," the Duke remarked sourly.

"My mother was your sister-in-law, married to your only brother," Kelvin Ward said quietly.

"If my brother had had any sense," the Duke retorted, "he would not have saddled himself with a wife and children, considering he was not in a position to support them."

Kelvin Ward's lips tightened and it was with an obvious effort that he forced himself not to argue with his Uncle but to continue what he was saying.

"A year later there was, as you know, an unfortunate incident involving my brother."

"A forger and a cheat!" the Duke said scathingly.

"Geoffrey was neither!" Kelvin Ward corrected. "He was weak and he got into the hands of unscrupulous men who encouraged him to gamble."

"A fool and his money are soon parted!" the Duke quoted with a mirthless laugh.

"In a moment of, I admit, complete madness," Kelvin Ward went on as if the Duke had not spoken, "Geoffrey forged the cheque of a brother Officer. Had the man in question been a gentleman he would have accepted the money from me and said no more about it."

"Instead he blackmailed you, eh?" the Duke asked, again with that mirthless attempt at a laugh.

"The whole incident cost me ten thousand pounds," Kelvin Ward said quietly. "I asked for your help at the time, if you remember, and you refused."

"Of course I refused." the Duke replied angrily. "Do you imagine I have nothing to do with my money but to throw it away on my relations who have not even a particle of honesty or decency in their make-up?"

"Are you including me in that condemnation?" Kelvin Ward asked.

The Duke hesitated a moment, and then as if he felt he had gone too far said:

"I met the Commander-in-Chief a month ago. He appears to think very highly of you."

"I am grateful!" Kelvin Ward said with a slight inclination of his head.

"He was apparently unaware that you intended to leave your Regiment."

"There was nothing else I could do," Kelvin Ward replied. "As I have just explained, sir, I owe fifteen thousand pounds, and it is impossible nowadays, even in India, for an Officer to live on his pay."

"You knew that when you wasted ten thousand pounds saving that reprobate brother of yours from the prison where he belonged."

"Geoffrey was killed performing an action of great gallantry on the North-West Frontier," Kelvin Ward said. "I see no point in defaming his memory."

The Duke snorted.

"All I can say," his nephew continued, "is that I am glad and I shall always be glad that his stupidity, for it was nothing more, was known to only a few people like yourself, and that the family name is still honoured at home and in the Regiment."

"Very high-falutin talk!" the Duke jeered. "But pretty words do not fill your pockets, as you have apparently found out for yourself!"

"The position is this . . ." Kelvin Ward went on.

He was speaking in the quiet, unemotional voice of a man who is determined not to lose his temper however greatly he is provoked.

His grey eyes in his thin sun-tanned face were

steely as he looked at his Uncle, but otherwise he did not betray in any way the fact that he was fighting for his future.

". . . I left the Regiment because I knew that not only was it impossible for me to afford it, but also because I have reached an age when I must make some provision for my future."

"I thought you were banking on my death," the Duke said with a sneer.

"At a conservative estimate," Kelvin Ward answered, "there is every likelihood of Your Grace living for another fifteen to twenty years. By that time I should be too old to start a new career."

His lips twisted in a wry smile as he added:

"While as things are at the moment, I should in the meantime starve."

"That is your business!" the Duke declared.

"I might point out to you," Kelvin Ward continued, "that in most noble families it is usual to allow the heir apparent to the title some small income so that he is not put to the straits of borrowing against his future."

There was a touch of irony in Kelvin Ward's voice, and the Duke said:

"As you have done, I presume?"

"With very good reason, Sir. But by no means all I needed. You have proclaimed your penury to all and sundry, so that the Usurers do not consider me a good risk."

"But you have tried?"

"Of course I have tried! The reason I was able to raise the five thousand pounds I required for my mother was their assumption that one day I would step into your shoes. But I had to find a guarantor for the ten thousand pounds to save Geoffrey. I cannot find another."

"Then I suggest you find other ways of raising the money you require," the Duke said.

"That is exactly what I am trying to do, Sir,"

Kelvin Ward said patiently, "if you will just hear me out."

"You are taking an unconscionable time in getting to the point," the Duke said sharply.

"Then I will make what I have to say as short as possible," Kelvin Ward promised." I have some acquaintances in Bombay who are buying two trading ships. As you must well know, the shipping of goods between India, England and Europe has been increasing year by year."

"I am not entirely deaf and blind about current events," the Duke retorted.

"Then you will have seen some of the figures which have been published in *The Times* and the *Morning Post*," Kelvin Ward said. "It is, I believe, the quickest and most honest manner in which to make money."

"So that is what you intend to do," the Duke interposed.

"If I could put up five thousand pounds I could become a partner—admittedly a very junior partner—of these acquaintances. They intend to plough back the profits year after year until they own a whole fleet."

"Very commendable!" the Duke said. "I hope you succeed in your aspirations."

"You know what I am asking, Sir."

"I have already given you the answer," the Duke replied. "I do not intend to dissipate my money—what little I have, and I assure you it is a mere pittance—on mad-cap schemes."

"You have just agreed that this is not a mad-cap scheme," Kelvin Ward interrupted.

". . . on mad-cap schemes," the Duke continued harshly, "run by harum-scarum young men without experience of anything except riding about on a charger and killing defenceless natives who do not possess weapons to defend themselves."

Kelvin Ward bit back the words that rose to his lips.

He had been two years on the North-West
Frontier where the tribesmen were equipped with
weapons provided by the Russians and used guer-
rilla tactics which took an unconscionable toll of
British lives. It was hard to hear his Uncle speak in
such a manner.

He had not, however, become an acknowledged
leader of men without learning how fatal it was to
lose one's temper.

"All I am asking you, Sir," he said, his voice as
expressionless as it had been before, "is to lend me
the money on a purely business-like basis."

The Duke did not speak and he continued:

"You will receive an annual dividend exactly
as if you had purchased a share on the Stock Mar-
ket, and I am absolutely confident that by the end
of our first trading year I shall be able to pay you
back some of your loan if not all of it."

"You are very optimistic!"

"You will help me?"

"No!" the Duke answered. "I cannot afford
it!"

Just for a moment Kelvin Ward was motion-
less.

He had an impulse to tell his Uncle exactly
what he thought of him but he knew it would only
result in an undignified scene from which he would
gain nothing.

After all, he told himself, he had not really anticipated that his Uncle would come to his assist-
ance.

The Duke had refused his pleadings when he
had almost gone down on his knees to ask him to
help his mother when she was dying.

He had never been able to forget the bitterness he had felt as he'd walked from Uxbridge
House with his Uncle's metallic voice echoing in
his ears.

"I have no use in my life for ailing women and
impecunious nephews!" he had shouted.

Kelvin Ward had been desperate then, and only by raising the money at an exorbitant rate of interest from the Usurers had he enabled Lady Ronald Ward to die in comfort.

Kelvin Ward rose to his feet.

"If that is your last word, Sir," he said, "then there is nothing more I can do to convince you."

"Nothing!" the Duke agreed. "You could have saved your time coming here and employed it better badgering someone else with your grandiose ideas!"

'Hardly grandiose!' Kelvin Ward thought to himself as he looked round the big, comfortable study.

He was sure that if he had a chance to search through the bookcases he would find many old volumes acquired by his ancestors which were first editions and therefore extremely valuable.

There were the portraits of the previous Dukes of Uxbridge hanging on the walls, some of which had been painted by world-famous artists.

Although he would not wish his Uncle to sell them, it was at the same time hard to accept the Duke's constant moan of poverty when he was surrounded by so many treasures.

Admittedly the carpets were threadbare and the linings of the damask curtains were in rags, the servants' livery was never renewed, and the Duke himself was known to be so parsimonious that it was a joke among his contemporaries.

'Is he really speaking the truth when he says that he is poverty-stricken?' Kelvin Ward asked himself.

It was a question which had been in his mind for many years, in fact ever since his father had died and he had become the heir to the Dukedom.

His Uncle had no intention of ever allowing his nephew any inside information about the family fortunes, nor had he at any time offered him any hospitality.

Kelvin Ward had not even been offered a glass of wine since he had arrived at Uxbridge House and there was no question of his ever having had a meal in his Uncle's company.

And yet he had come back from India in optimistic mood.

He had told himself that his Uncle might just for once help him to make a living.

It had been a wrench to leave the Regiment. Even now he could hardly bear to think of the soldiers he had trained and commanded without a pain in his heart that was almost like a wound.

He had abandoned his Army career, as he had told his Uncle, only because he faced the cold, hard truth that he could not live on his pay. To get deeper and deeper into debt was against his character, his whole code of behaviour.

"I believe Kelvin Ward is the most incorruptible man I have ever met," he had heard the Colonel of the Regiment say once when he did not know he was within hearing.

And yet now he wondered wryly if that epithet would apply to him in the future.

He had decided to go into commerce, to become a trader, and he was well aware that his accepted ethics of honour and integrity were not exactly the qualities which carried one quickly along the road to wealth.

The acquaintances of whom he had spoken to the Duke were very keen for him to join them.

"You are exactly the man we want," one of them had said. "People trust you instantly, Ward, and today where business is concerned that is very important."

Now it seemed to Kelvin Ward there was no chance of his entering the business world. His whole future seemed to be blank, and for the moment he had no ideas about dealing with it.

He left Uxbridge House having said a polite

good-bye to his Uncle, and without showing any rancour or ill-feeling.

"What did you give me—fifteen years?" the Duke asked jeeringly as a parting shot. "Well, I shall try to make it twenty-five just to spite you, Kelvin! It would be a mistake for you to change all the stringent economies I have made on the Estates."

Kelvin Ward was sure his Uncle was trying to provoke him into saying something he might later regret, so did not give him the satisfaction of a reply.

Instead he bowed and, having left Uxbridge House, walked in the cold sharp air through Mayfair towards his Club in St. James's.

Deep in his thoughts, he had no idea that practically every woman he passed turned her head to look back at him.

It was not only that he was very elegant and what was known as a 'fine figure of a man.' It was his strength of personality, something that made everyone he met instantly aware of his presence.

When he reached his Club, Kelvin Ward went into the Morning-Room and threw himself down into a deep leather arm-chair.

He wondered as he did so how long he could afford the subscription which he had to pay if he was to remain a member, and decided that at the moment, although he needed one, he could not afford to buy himself a drink.

"What is the matter, Kelvin? You look hipped," a familiar voice said as his friend Sir Anthony Fanshawe lowered himself into an adjacent chair.

"I am!"

"What has happened?"

"I have been with my Uncle."

"The cheese-paring Duke is enough to throw anyone into a despondency. I imagine that he said he could not help you?"

"He was very positive he would not!"

"I never expected him to say anything else," Sir Anthony said. "My father, who knew him all his life, often said when he was alive that if the Duke saw someone bleeding to death by the roadside he would pass quickly in case it should cost him anything to stop."

"Your father was right!" Kelvin said briefly.

"What are you going to do?" Sir Anthony enquired.

"I have not the slightest idea!"

"Will you have a drink?"

"If you can afford one."

"I can stand you that," Sir Anthony said with a smile and put up his hand to the waiter.

An hour later they were still sitting in the Morning-Room and while they had discussed every possibility there seemed to be no-where they could turn to find the money that Kelvin Ward so urgently required.

"I suppose I have been a fool!" he said at one moment. "Other men come back from India complete Nabobs, jingling their ill-gotten gains. There are ways out there of making money, as you well know, Anthony."

"I cannot see you stooping to them," his friend replied.

"Beggars cannot afford pride," Kelvin said bitterly.

"If you of all people had done those sort of things," Sir Anthony said, "it would have reacted on the whole Regiment. You know that as well as I do."

"That is exactly why I did not do them," Kelvin Ward said, "but that does not help me at the moment."

"We will think of something," his friend said consolingly. "If I had the money I would give it to you, you know that!"

Kelvin Ward smiled.

"You are the best friend I ever had, Anthony, but unfortunately you too are in debt. If only I could get this shipping business going you could come in with me."

"There must be someone you can approach," Sir Anthony said, knitting his brow.

"I have thought of everyone," Kelvin replied. "Having been out of England for so long, I have lost touch with most people I knew well, and being my Uncle's nephew does not exactly help matters!"

Without saying more they were both aware that the Duke had made more enemies than almost any man in the country.

Everyone disliked him. Everyone deplored and denounced the meanness with which he had treated his brother, Kelvin's father, who had been very popular. And worse still, the manner in which he had ignored and neglected his sister-in-law after her husband's death.

There was practically no-one who had not a tale of some sort to tell against the Duke.

He had never been known to give a penny to charity. He treated his employees on the Estate with a meanness that was even denounced in the newspapers.

He was not only a miser, but a spiteful and vindictive one, and it was true to say that he had not a friend in the world.

"What are you going to do this evening?" Sir Anthony asked after their conversation seemed to pause for lack of new ideas for raising money.

"I cannot afford to do anything!" Kelvin Ward replied. "I was a fool to waste what ready money I had in coming back from India. I should have stayed out there and seen if there was any chance of getting a decently paid job."

"There are not many for men like you," Sir Anthony said gloomily.

They both knew this was true.

It was impossible to visualise Kelvin Ward becoming a clerk in the East India Company or hiring himself out to a commercial firm.

"For Heaven's sake! Let us have another drink!" Sir Anthony said.

A waiter approached them, but it was not in answer to his raised hand. Instead the man held out a silver salver towards Kelvin Ward.

There was a letter on it.

He looked at it in surprise.

"When did this come?"

"It has just been brought by hand, Sir. A groom is waiting for your answer."

Sir Anthony looked at the white envelope with curiosity—and teased his friend:

"Some fair charmer must know you are in London."

Kelvin Ward did not answer. He was reading the letter with a puzzled expression on his face.

"Ask the groom to wait a moment," he said to the waiter.

"Very good, Sir."

The waiter went away and Kelvin Ward said:

"What do you know of Sir Erasmus Malton?"

"Is that who has written to you?"

"Yes," Kelvin Ward replied, "but I do not understand it."

"What does the letter say?"

Kelvin Ward handed the sheet of heavy and expensive writing-paper to his friend. Sir Anthony took it and read it.

> Sir Erasmus Malton presents his compliments to Major Kelvin Ward and would like to see him on a matter which will be to Major Ward's advantage.

"Now what the devil does that mean?" Kelvin Ward asked.

"Anything that Sir Erasmus could do for you would certainly be to your advantage."

"I seem to know the name but I cannot place it."

"I suppose Sir Erasmus is one of the richest men in England," Sir Anthony informed him. "At the same time, he is rather a mystery. No-one seems to be quite sure how he made so much money, but he certainly possesses it and he seems to have a finger in every pie."

"Is he a gentleman?"

"I really do not know, but I think so. No-one has ever suggested he is not, but I do not move in the same society as tycoons and millionaires, and that is where Sir Erasmus is to be found."

"Then what can he want with me?" Kelvin Ward enquired.

"I imagine he is going to offer you a job," Sir Anthony replied.

"But he has never met me. Now that I think about it, I have heard of him. Not only here in England, but in India. What was it I was told?"

"That he is rich as Croesus, I expect," Sir Anthony said. "I have heard my cousin, the Foreign Secretary, speaking of him. I believe he is rather impressed by Sir Erasmus. I will find out more when he comes back from Paris."

"In the meantime I have to answer this note."

"Then what are you waiting for? Accept if nothing else. Smell money and hope that some of the gold-dust will rub off on you!"

Kelvin Ward looked at the clock on the mantelpiece.

"Shall I say I will call on him within the hour? It might look as if I were inviting myself to dinner."

"Well at least you would not have to buy your own meal," Sir Anthony remarked laconically.

"That is certainly a major inducement to make me accept Sir Erasmus's invitation," Kelvin Ward said with a laugh.

He rose from his chair and walked towards a

writing-table. He wrote a few lines, enclosed the
sheet in an envelope and, calling the waiter, told
him to take it to the groom waiting outside.

"The die is cast!" he said as he went back to
his friend. "Now what will fate produce?"

"Perhaps you will discover that Sir Erasmus is
your long-lost god-father. He will make you his
heir and disappear in a cloud of smoke!" Sir Anthony joked.

"I only hope your prediction comes true!"
Kelvin Ward said. "But I have the dismal convic-
tion there is nothing in this but perhaps an invitation to a Social Soirée or an obligation to propel an
unfledged débutante round a Ball-Room."

"God forbid!" Sir Anthony said piously.

"Amen to that!" Kelvin Ward smiled.

A little over an hour later Kelvin Ward was
ushered into a Library twice the size and a hundred
times more impressive than that in which he had
conversed with his Uncle.

He had not known quite what he expected
when he had taken a hackney-carriage to Malton
House in Park Lane.

The name of the mansion had been changed
ten years ago when Sir Erasmus had bought it.

Before that it had belonged to a nobleman who
on his death bed omitted to leave enough money
for his heirs to continue living in the grandeur to
which they had been accustomed.

It was obvious to Kelvin Ward that a huge
sum of money must have been spent on redecorat-
ing and refurbishing what had been an impressive
but undoubtedly dilapidated building.

He admired the painted ceiling in the entrance
hall from which hung gigantic chandeliers, and saw
on the walls a profusion of valuable paintings
which were enough to make a connoisseur of the
Arts open his eyes in surprise long before he en-
countered his host.

Kelvin Ward had been trained in the Army to notice detail and he did not fail to appraise the thickness of the carpet in the Library, the Genoese velvet which curtained the windows and the unique Objects d'Art on the side-tables.

The owner of such magnificence was certainly more impressive than his Uncle.

Sir Erasmus Malton was a man with a distinct and undeniable personality. His features were refined and there was no doubt he was in fact a gentleman.

Kelvin Ward, who had half-expected to meet a self-made tycoon who had risen up the social ladder from the gutter, was pleasantly surprised by Sir Erasmus's cultured voice and firm handshake as he said:

"It is good of you to come and see me at such short notice, Major Ward."

Kelvin Ward inclined his head and Sir Erasmus indicated a chair in front of a finely carved marble fireplace.

"You had a pleasant journey back from India?" Sir Erasmus asked, crossing his legs.

"The ship was not full," Kelvin Ward replied, "so I did not have to be too social."

"That on shipboard is undoubtedly a blessing," Sir Erasmus smiled.

The Butler, attended by two footmen, proffered Kelvin Ward several different sorts of wine, and there were pâté sandwiches in a crested silver dish.

As the servants left the room Sir Erasmus said:

"You must be wondering why I wished to see you."

"I admit to feeling extremely curious," Kelvin Ward replied.

"You may be even more surprised by what I have to say," Sir Erasmus said slowly. "I have been following your career, Major Ward, for several years."

Kelvin Ward looked startled.

"In what way?"

"I heard about you and I wished to learn more," Sir Erasmus said. "I know of your distinguished career in the Army, that you have been decorated and have won the admiration of your Senior Officers."

"Thank you," Kelvin Ward said. "It is always pleasant to hear complimentary things about one's self, but I cannot understand why it should interest you."

"I am coming to that," Sir Erasmus said. "What I want you to realise is that I have given you a great deal of thought. I have also learnt of the part you played in saving your brother from being discredited."

Kelvin Ward sat up abruptly.

"How could you have known that?"

"I have a way of learning things about the people who interest me," Sir Erasmus said so quietly that it did not sound like boasting.

Kelvin Ward was silent.

He was indeed perturbed that an outsider should have learnt of Geoffrey's dishonesty. He had hoped that very few people indeed were aware of what had happened.

"I also know," Sir Erasmus went on, "that by his death your brother most admirably made reparation for the past."

"Thank you," Kelvin Ward said again.

"But your part in what was undoubtedly a very unsavoury incident I felt was very commendable," Sir Erasmus continued, "and I also thought it courageous of you to leave your Regiment knowing that you could not afford to stay on."

"How can you know all this about me?" Kelvin Ward enquired.

"I know more," Sir Erasmus answered. "I am

aware that you came back to England hoping to persuade your Uncle to finance your plans for venturing into the world of commerce."

"I cannot imagine . . ." Kelvin Ward began, only to be interrupted by his host, who finished:

". . . I think I am also right in my assumption that the Duke has refused to help you."

"You do not have to be clairvoyant to guess that!" Kelvin Ward said in a hard voice.

"Therefore I imagine you have not yet formed plans for the immediate future."

"When your note came to the Club," Kelvin Ward answered, "I was sitting with a friend trying to find a solution to my problems."

"That is why I have asked you here," Sir Erasmus said. "I have a proposition to put to you, Major Ward, which I think you will find interesting."

"There is no need for me to say, Sir, that I shall be only too glad to listen to anything which might assist me at the moment."

Sir Erasmus paused for a moment as if he was choosing his words.

At the same time Kelvin Ward was well aware that he was in complete command of the situation.

There was no doubt that he was an extremely clever and astute man. There was something about his high forehead, the sharpness of his eyes, even in the way he moved, which bespoke a man who could, if he wished, command an Empire.

Only to look at him, Kelvin Ward felt, was to realise that he would reach the top whatever the difficulties. There was a force and a power about him and he did not doubt that he could, if he wished, be very ruthless.

"I have made enquiries about you for a special reason," Sir Erasmus said, "which has not been idle curiosity. Indeed I would not have time for such trivialities. I will say quite frankly that I have also made enquiries about other men of your age."

His voice was impressive as he said:

"Without flattering you, Major Ward, I consider you at this present time to be easily the most outstanding young man in Society."

"In Society?" Kelvin Ward questioned with a smile. "That hardly applies to me. I have been out of England for the last four years, and even when I was here I had neither the inclination nor the means to cut a dash in the social world."

"We are speaking of rather different things," Sir Erasmus said coldly. "I am referring to your social status. You are of the nobility, your family is part of our history, and you are the heir to a Dukedom."

"And a great deal of good it does me at the moment!" Kelvin Ward remarked bitterly.

"Nevertheless when your Uncle dies, as die he must like the rest of us, you will become the Duke of Uxbridge!"

Kelvin Ward did not answer and Sir Erasmus continued:

"Not only because of those assets, but because I consider your character, your personality and your behaviour to be exemplary in every way, I am suggesting that I can help you very considerably in the project in which you are interested."

"It is exceedingly kind of you," Kelvin Ward said. "As you know so much you are doubtless aware that I saw my Uncle today and asked him to lend me, entirely as a business proposition, five thousand pounds. With this money I could become a junior partner with some acquaintances who, with two ships, intend to start trading from Bombay."

"I know all that," Sir Erasmus said with a touch of impatience, "but it was not five thousand pounds that I envisaged as your collateral but that you should have the handling of something like three hundred thousand!"

Kelvin Ward drew in his breath.

"If somebody had said this to me yesterday," he said, "I would have thought it a joke."

"It is certainly no joke," Sir Erasmus said, "but there is of course one condition attached to my proposition."

"And what is that?" Kelvin Ward enquired.

"It is," Sir Erasmus said gravely, "that you should marry my daughter!"

For a moment there was a silence in the room. Then Kelvin Ward said incredulously:

"Are you speaking seriously?"

"Do I sound otherwise?" Sir Erasmus enquired. "I must explain to you that not only am I a man of determination, but I plan any campaign in which I am involved down to the smallest detail."

He paused a moment, then went on:

"It must be obvious to you therefore that I would choose my daughter's husband and my future son-in-law with the care and perception that I should employ in a business deal."

He added impressively:

"I can only say that you are the only man I could consider seriously in this respect."

"I am of course flattered!" Kelvin Ward replied gravely, "but are you not, Sir, being somewhat precipitate? Perhaps if I could meet the young lady in question and we grew to like each other, then there might be a chance if we found each other compatible that things could be as you wish."

He spoke very carefully, having no wish to offend Sir Erasmus but feeling in a way shocked at the idea which had been presented to him so unexpectedly.

He had never for a moment imagined that he would hear a suggestion so fantastic and almost outrageous from a man of Sir Erasmus's standing.

What was more, he had no intention of getting

married and certainly not to a woman of someone else's choice.

But he was too shrewd to offend Sir Erasmus, who was obviously sincere and who, he was well aware, could help him if he wished to do so.

"I understood," Sir Erasmus replied, "that it was important for you to return to India with the money immediately and that your associates have given you a time limit before they look elsewhere for funds."

"You are correct in that assumption," Kelvin Ward said, "but at the same time I can hardly believe you are serious in suggesting that I should agree to marry a girl whom I have never seen and who might take a dislike to me on sight."

"That is not your reputation where women are concerned," Sir Erasmus said, "and I cannot believe, Major Ward, that you are so obtuse as not to see the advantages of marriage with my only child."

Kelvin Ward did not reply and he said:

"In case you are thinking she might not be suitable for the rank you will hold on your Uncle's death, I should perhaps tell you something about myself."

"It is not really necessary," Kelvin Ward murmured.

"I should consider it very necessary if I were in your place," Sir Erasmus replied. "As I have already told you, in business every detail is of the utmost importance. I therefore wish to inform you that in my own ancestry I have nothing of which I need be ashamed."

He looked up at one of the portraits on the wall as he went on:

"There have been Maltons in Yorkshire, and they have been considerable land-owners, since the sixteenth century.

"My wife was the daughter of the Earl of Kilkenny, and when we married we could, if we had wished, have taken our place in Society, which in view of my wealth would undoubtedly have welcomed us with open arms."

There was a touch of irony in Sir Erasmus's voice.

"But my wife was in delicate health and she did not wish for gaieties or entertainments. She was content to stay in the country while I came to London to deal with my business affairs. When she died, I had no-one left to care for but our daughter."

Just for a moment it seemed there was a touch of emotion in the calm voice, but Major Ward could not be sure of it.

"Seraphina is now eighteen," Sir Erasmus continued. "She has been brought up in the way my wife had chosen for her. She has been educated very widely by Governesses and Tutors. Otherwise she has lived a quiet and simple existence."

His voice hardened as he added:

"I have no desire for her to be pursued by fortune-hunters."

"No, of course not," Kelvin Ward murmured as he realised that he was expected to say something.

"I therefore decided over five years ago that when the time came for Seraphina to be married, I would choose her husband for her," Sir Erasmus went on.

"Women are usually beguiled and fascinated by the most unsuitable men, especially young women! I have no intention of seeing my daughter captivated and my wealth dissipated by some money-greedy Romeo."

"I can understand that," Kelvin Ward said.

"It therefore seemed sensible for me," Sir Erasmus continued, "to choose the man I wanted to handle my fortune when I am dead."

"Has your daughter no say in whom she marries?" Kelvin Ward enquired.

"Most young girls have little say in such matters," Sir Erasmus replied.

Kelvin Ward knew that this was true enough. If the average society girl received a good offer or a suitable *parti* approached her father, she would undoubtedly be pressured into marriage whether she wished it or not.

There was a silence and then Sir Erasmus asked:

"Well?"

"Have I to give you my answer now?" Kelvin Ward enquired.

"Perhaps I should show you something first."

Sir Erasmus rose to his feet and walked to a large desk which stood in the centre of the room.

It was flat-topped and on it rested a gold inkpot which Kelvin Ward recognised as being a fine example of the craftmanship of the Reign of Charles II.

He looked at it with interest, appreciating the exquisite workmanship, as Sir Erasmus drew some papers from a drawer and laid them out in front of him.

Kelvin Ward took a quick look at them and was very still.

"Where did you get those?"

"I bought them," Sir Erasmus answered. "Usurers usually have a price for such things."

Kelvin Ward bit back the words that came to his lips.

It seemed incredible that he should be in debt not to a firm of Money Lenders, as he had fancied, but to Sir Erasmus Malton!

Yet in front of him lay the receipts he had signed and with them slips showing that he had paid the exorbitant rate of interest on the dates required of him.

"As soon as you agree to my suggestion," Sir Erasmus said slowly, "these papers are of course consigned to the flames."

"And if I do not?" Kelvin Ward asked sharply.

Sir Erasmus paused for a moment.

"You really wish me to put it into words?" he enquired.

There was no need.

Kelvin Ward knew that he was being threatened, and it was one of the most unpleasant sensations he had ever experienced in his life.

He had the feeling that he was facing a man so ruthless, so utterly determined upon getting his own way, that he would stop at nothing.

Kelvin Ward was well aware what it would mean if he were to be made bankrupt, which Sir Erasmus could achieve just by asking for repayment.

It would mean what he had always tried to avoid—dishonour to the family name!

It would also mean that he must resign from his Clubs so that he would not meet the few friends that he had left.

It would doubly ensure that his chances of entering the business world would be nil.

Even in India traders were wary and looked askance at men who were bankrupt, however socially eligible they might be. And he knew that he himself would loathe and detest the stigma of it.

For the second time that day Kelvin Ward was fighting for control of his feelings.

For the second time he told himself that nothing could be gained by losing his temper, and yet he could feel a black rage rising inside him.

He disliked being manipulated. He disliked more than he could possibly express not to have freedom of choice, not to be his own master.

And yet here in an incredible fashion he was faced with a choice of only two possibilities—one of marrying a woman he had never seen and becoming the son-in-law of a man he already disliked; the other, of having his debts called in and facing bankruptcy.

He wondered wildly if he could once again approach his Uncle. Then he knew that he could not expect any help from that direction.

The Duke had been prepared to let his sister-in-law die without raising a finger to save her. He certainly would not spend a penny on keeping his nephew from the Court of Bankruptcy.

It seemed to Kelvin Ward as if he were completely surrounded by a superior enemy, and he could not fight his way out.

"You asked me just now," Sir Erasmus continued, "whether I required your answer to my question immediately. I do!"

Kelvin Ward looked again at the evidence of his debts spread out on the desk.

Sir Erasmus watched him with what he thought was a faintly cynical smile in his hard eyes.

Then he said in a voice which he was gratified to find was quiet and steady:

"As you are aware, I have no alternative. I will marry your daughter!"

Chapter Two

Kelvin Ward looked round the vast Dining-Room of Malton House with a feeling of active dislike.

He had been in a black rage since he had risen that morning and remembered it was his wedding-day.

It would have been difficult for him to forget it, because for the last three days he had been concerned with nothing else.

Even now he could hardly credit that Sir Erasmus had required him to be married within three days of their first conversation, and that to-morrow morning he and his bride would be leaving for India.

Sir Erasmus had told him that for him every detail of anything he undertook was important, but Kelvin Ward had not at that moment realised that it was an obsession.

Sir Erasmus left nothing to chance.

Everything was planned, directed, ordered and arranged so that life became a mathematical sum which must add up to the correct total.

From the moment that Kelvin Ward had said, "I will marry your daughter," it was as if he set a monster machine into operation.

Sir Erasmus had first of all picked up the bills and receipts from the desk and walked across the room to throw them into the fire.

Kelvin Ward watched them burning without the feeling of satisfaction which he knew he should have felt.

He was only uncomfortably aware that he had passed from being a debtor of the Usurers into what he surmised would be much more tenacious and inescapable hands.

It was difficult for him to explain to his friend Sir Anthony Fanshawe, who was waiting for his return to the Club, the violent distaste he already felt for the whole transaction.

"Good God, Kelvin! What are you complaining about?" Sir Anthony enquired. "If anyone has fallen on their feet it is you!"

"I can imagine nothing worse than having to marry the daughter of a man to whom I have taken an intense dislike and whose only interest in me is that one day I shall wear a Ducal coronet."

"I would marry Medusa herself if she brought with her a dowry of three hundred thousand and the anticipation of millions!" Sir Anthony said.

"If my mythology is not at fault," Kelvin Ward replied, "Medusa's hair consisted of snakes, reptiles for which having lived in India I have a strong aversion."

"Do not damn the girl before you see her," Sir Anthony pleaded.

"Can you not see that it is an intolerable situation to be in?" Kelvin Ward asked. "I had not thought of marriage. Who could have in my circumstances? But I imagined that when I did marry, I would find someone with whom I could settle down in peace and happiness. I can assure you I

had not contemplated a woman with a father like
Sir Erasmus!"

"I cannot help admiring his perspicacity and
his determination!" Sir Anthony said. "Fancy taking the trouble of delving into your life, and for all
we know into the lives of perhaps dozens of other
men, to find exactly the type of son-in-law with
whom he could entrust his vast fortune!"

"I do not want his money!" Kelvin Ward exclaimed. "All I want is enough to have a chance to
make my own way in the world. To prove myself!"

"Five thousand pounds in fact!" Sir Anthony
said with a smile.

"That is what I asked for."

"I think you are biased against your future
father-in-law," Sir Anthony said, "and that is unlike you, Kelvin. I have never known you to be
anything but just and fair."

"Perhaps that is because I have always been
coping with other people's problems," Kelvin Ward
remarked. "It is difficult to feel objective and unbi-
ased when one is caught like a rat in a trap."

It was a simile he was to apply to himself fre-
quently during the next two days.

He had to visit Sir Erasmus the following
morning and found several Attorneys with him.

He was shown the deeds and investments
which constituted Seraphina Malton's fortune, of
which her father wished him to have the handling
from the moment they were married.

He was in many ways surprised that Sir Erasmus intended to retain no authority whatsoever
over his daughter's wealth, but would allow it to be
administered as the law decreed as in the case of
every other married woman, by her husband from
the moment she took his name.

"This is what my daughter already possesses,"
Sir Erasmus said.

Kelvin Ward perused the documents that were
handed to him.

"I intend to set aside the sum of one million pounds," Sir Erasmus continued, "to form a Trust for the children of the marriage. Each will take possession of his share of this fund on reaching the age of twenty-five. In the meantime you will be the sole Trustee."

"I think it would be far better for you to administer it yourself," Kelvin Ward said.

"I have already made my arrangements," Sir Erasmus answered coldly. "If I did not consider you competent to handle large sums I should not have suggested it."

There was nothing more Kelvin Ward could say.

At the same time he felt again that surge of resentment that he was being bound hand and foot to the wheels of Sir Erasmus's juggernaut.

The more he learned about his future father-in-law's affairs, the more astonished he became that any man could have built up such a far-reaching business which apparently extended all over the world.

He was like an octopus, Kelvin Ward thought, sucking up profits with tentacles which crept into the most unlikely places and into the most obscure of schemes.

Wherever there was a profit to be made, Sir Erasmus was there.

Looking round the Dining-Room where over a hundred people were seated to partake of an Epicurean wedding-breakfast, Kelvin Ward wondered how many millions of pounds were represented under the painted ceiling.

When Sir Erasmus had told him that the wedding was to take place on the third day of their acquaintance, it had sounded in some ways a sensible arrangement.

"The Steam Ship *Tiberius* is leaving Tilbury for Bombay the following morning," Sir Erasmus said. "I will book you what is known as 'The Bridal

Suite.' I understand the ship is larger and more comfortable than any other leaving the following week."

There could be nothing for Kelvin Ward to do but agree.

He imagined that this would mean that the wedding would be a very quiet one. After all, he told himself, there was hardly time for the bride to pack, let alone invite a large congregation to witness their nuptials.

He had, however, reckoned without Sir Erasmus.

Telegrams were dispatched. Grooms had distributed the invitations inscribed by Sir Erasmus's secretaries, and acceptances poured in.

When Sir Erasmus showed Kelvin Ward the list of guests who had been invited he was astonished to see how important they were, not only in the world of finance but in Parliamentary and to some extent social circles.

There were, it was true, none of the frivolous pleasure-loving people who circled round the Prince of Wales and were known as the 'Marlborough House Set.'

But there were Statesmen who bore household names, Members both of the House of Lords and the House of Commons who had made their mark, and while the Prime Minister the Marquess of Salisbury was too busy his wife had accepted.

Besides these Kelvin Ward could see that all the great Bankers, the cosmopolitan Financiers, the men on whom European Governments relied when a National loan was required, were to be present.

One conspicuous absentee was the Duke of Uxbridge, but Kelvin Ward had received a note from him. It consisted of two words—"How sensible."

The majority of the guests had of course brought their wives, but there were in fact more men than women seated round the long orchid-decorated tables.

The food consisted of delicacies which were so exotic and so expensive that even one of them would have kept the average working man's family in luxury for a month.

The wines were superlative—a different one for each course—and because he felt that perhaps it would lift the depression which seemed to envelop him like a fog, Kelvin Ward drank more than he usually allowed himself to do.

But it was no use.

Nothing could disperse the rage he had felt on rising, and the anger which made it hard for him not only to concentrate on anything people were saying but even to focus his eyes.

He had not believed that Sir Erasmus was serious when he had said after discussing Seraphina's investments that he was not to meet his bride until they stood side by side in front of the altar.

"I hope I may have the pleasure of meeting Miss Malton today," Kelvin Ward had said politely.

"Seraphina is in the country," Sir Erasmus replied, "and she will not be coming to London until the night before the wedding."

"I shall not meet her then?"

"No!" Sir Erasmus answered. "There is nothing you could say to each other that I cannot say for you."

"But really—" Kelvin Ward began.

Then he checked the words of protest which hovered on his lips.

'Let Sir Erasmus have it his own way,' he told himself. 'He is a dictator, and it is doubtful that anything I say or do will make him change his plans. Therefore I may as well be silent.'

It was only to Sir Anthony that he let off steam.

"The man is inhuman!" he exclaimed. "Can

you imagine any father ordering his child into marriage as if she were a blind-folded cow?"

"I dare say the girl is perfectly prepared to believe what her father has told her about you," Sir Anthony said. "You are a very presentable young man, Kelvin, especially to the female sex."

That was true and Kelvin Ward did not attempt to deny it.

He would have lied if he had pretended he did not know that women were fascinated by him and that any woman to whom he paid attention was only too ready to reciprocate.

At the same time his love affairs, and there had been a great many of them, had all been with either married women or widows! Sophisticated, witty, intelligent women who knew how to play the game from a provocative flirtation to a grand but discreet passion.

"What the hell am I to say to a girl who is hardly out of the School-Room?" he asked Sir Anthony.

"I cannot help you there," his friend replied. "I never speak to girls if I can help it."

"I cannot even remember when I last danced with one, let alone talked to the species," Kelvin Ward said.

"Surely there are plenty of them in India." Sir Anthony remarked. "I have always understood they are known as the 'Fishing Fleet.' "

"They are!" Kelvin Ward smiled, "and as I have never envisaged myself on a hook, I have made every effort to avoid them!"

He paused and added:

"Only to be brought to the gaff by an astute and very experienced angler!"

"Cheer up!" Sir Anthony answered. "It may not be as bad as you think. At least the girl should have some intelligence if she is anything like her father.

"It is just because I am afraid she will be like

her father," Kelvin Ward answered, "that I would
rather face an Army of Amazons than Miss Seraphina Malton!"

Kelvin Ward told himself that he was sure
that one of the reasons for Sir Erasmus's haste in
tying the knot was the fear that even at the elev-
enth hour he might find some way of escaping from
the net in which he had been caught.

But while he had played with the idea of running away he knew in fact it was impossible.

Where could he find fifteen thousand pounds
to pay the debts that Sir Erasmus had thrown on
the fire but which still remained a commitment of
honour?

And if he did not have the money to invest in
the shipping project waiting for him at Bombay,
where could he find employment or even enough
money just to keep himself alive?

'No—there is nothing I can do but behave with
dignity,' Kelvin Ward told himself when he was
dressed and ready for his wedding.

But all the resolutions in the world could not
prevent his hating every moment of it, loathing his
father-in-law and being convinced that he would
dislike his wife on sight.

It was rather difficult to see what she looked
like when finally she came up the aisle of the
Grosvenor Chapel on Sir Erasmus's arm.

She was dressed conventionally in white and
carried a bouquet of white orchids which seemed
over-large and opulent.

A large veil covered her face, and at a quick
sideways glance all Kelvin Ward saw was a bowed
head and a huge, sparkling diamond tiara which he
thought proclaimed almost vulgarly her monetary
value.

It was certainly, he thought, from the bridegroom's point of view, the cheapest marriage in
which any man could take part.

He had at least expected to purchase the wedding-ring, but a note from Sir Erasmus informed him that Seraphina would wear her mother's.

It was enclosed in a velvet box.

Wedding-presents, most of them very valuable and expensive, poured into Malton House.

Kelvin Ward glanced at them perfunctorily because it was expected of him, and he learned that they were being acknowledged by one of Sir Erasmus's secretaries.

They seemed as they glittered and sparkled as cold and impersonal as the wedding itself.

In fact he had nothing to do but acquiesce in Sir Erasmus's plans.

It therefore did not much surprise him when they left Grosvenor Chapel to find that Sir Erasmus was travelling with them in the bridal-carriage.

It was but three-minutes' drive to Malton House, but Kelvin Ward wondered with a wry smile whether Sir Erasmus had any ulterior motive in ensuring that the 'happy pair' were not in a position to exchange even a word together without his chaperonage.

As it was, no-one spoke except Sir Erasmus.

"A very pleasant ceremony," he said. "I think my choice of prayers very appropriate and the hymns—also of my choosing—were well rendered by the choir."

Kelvin Ward wanted to ask if he had also directed Almighty God to give them His blessing, but he doubted if Sir Erasmus would appreciate the sarcasm.

At Malton House the bride and bridegroom stood just inside the Salon, where a bower of highly scented and exotic lilies had been arranged as a background for them to receive the guests who arrived almost as soon as they did.

A stentorian voice announced each newcomer and Kelvin Ward found himself looking with interest at many people who had until now been only

names he had read about in the newspaper headlines or on the financial page.

Sir Erasmus had arranged that the wedding
ceremony should take place at four o'clock in the
afternoon, and it was not until after ten o'clock
that the long, drawn-out, so-called 'Wedding-
Breakfast' came to an end and they rose from the
table in the Dining-Room.

There had been speeches, but they were short.
A toast was drunk to the bride and bridegroom
before the coffee was brought to the tables and the
port and liqueurs were offered round.

It was a few minutes later that Kelvin Ward
realised that his bride was no longer at his side.

He had been talking or rather listening to the
Lord Chancellor, Lord Halsbury, on his right
speaking about the aims of the new Government
after the recent General Election.

The Lord Chancellor turned to speak to the
lady on his other side and Kelvin Ward found that
the chair next to him was empty.

Seraphina had slipped quietly away and when
as he would have asked for an explanation, Sir
Erasmus said:

"My daughter has a head-ache. She left you
her apologies."

"I expect she found it rather an ordeal," Kelvin Ward said automatically.

He knew that for him it had been an experience that he would never willingly repeat.

The ladies left the room and the gentlemen lit
their cigars.

The wedding-party became like the end of any
ordinary dinner with the gentlemen discussing the
topics which interested them most or amusing each
other with rather warm stories.

Kelvin Ward saw Sir Anthony laughing
uproariously at some tale one of the guests had
told him, but he himself felt only the same black
anger that had possessed him all day.

Finally the last guests said good-bye and even Sir Erasmus himself left.

It was another of his arrangements with which there had been no arguing that it would be quite absurd for his daughter and her husband to leave her home at which the wedding-breakfast had been held to stay at some uncomfortable Hotel for the night.

They had to leave for Tilbury at about ten o'clock the next morning, and there was no necessity to be in unfamiliar surroundings until they departed.

Sir Erasmus himself therefore had arranged to leave Malton House to stay with one of his rich and influential friends whose equally ornate mansion was also situated in Park Lane.

'Whether he is here or not,' Kelvin Ward thought savagely, 'his influence and the atmosphere he creates will remain!'

He could imagine nothing more unromantic than to spend the first night of one's marriage in the vast treasure-house, which was almost a mausoleum, on which Sir Erasmus had implanted indelibly his personality.

Yet again he had not argued but accepted the arrangements which had been made.

There was only one welcome thought, which was that after tomorrow he would no longer be in the vicinity of his father-in-law.

There would soon be a whole Continent and ocean between them, and Kelvin Ward had already decided that he would not return to England until he was his own master.

Until he could command his own destiny and need no longer be a slave who must do Sir Erasmus's bidding, he would remain abroad.

As the front door closed behind Sir Erasmus, Kelvin Ward found himself alone except for several flunkeys in the great marble Hall.

He turned to walk slowly up the curving stair-

case to the suite which he had learnt had been allotted to him and his wife.

He had already seen his own room, which was
extremely impressive. It opened into a boudoir, on
the other side of which was the bed-room occupied
by Seraphina.

There was the fragrance of lilies and carna-
tions as Kelvin Ward opened the door of the
boudoir and crossed the thick carpet into his own
room to find a valet waiting for him.

He wanted now, as he had wanted all day, to
be alone, and yet even when the door shut behind
the servant, he still felt crowded and on edge as if
a host of people encompassed him.

It was then that the blazing anger that he had
tried to keep under control seemed to surge up
within him and make him feel as if he were on fire.

He thought to himself he had never been
through such torture as he had suffered these last
three days, feeling that Sir Erasmus had taken him
over body, mind and soul.

He was no longer himself but a puppet which
must dance as his father-in-law directed.

Kelvin Ward was very proud. He was also exceedingly intelligent.

He told himself that having accepted the inev-
itable, he must make the best of it.

But every drop of blood in his veins rebelled
against the fact that he had been forced into a situation which he loathed and which struck at his
very manhood.

Always he had been a leader. Ever since he
had been a boy at school others had looked to him
to command; to control; to inspire.

Where another man would have accepted
phlegmatically this situation, to Kelvin Ward, because of the strength of his personality, it was intolerable.

Slowly he undressed, conscious all the time
that his bride was waiting for him.

He anticipated that she might be resentful that he had been detained so long.

If she was like her father she would have everything planned. It was also likely that she would be possessive, dictatorial, perhaps even aggressive.

'I will not be bossed by my wife,' Kelvin Ward told himself grimly.

He foresaw battles ahead, but battles in which he intended to be the victor from the very start. He squared his chin.

Then he realised with something akin to horror that he had not the slightest idea what Seraphina looked like.

Could the reason for Sir Erasmus not allowing him to see her before they were united in wedlock be that she was deformed or repulsive?

He felt stricken at the thought!

He had vaguely imagined that she would resemble her father and be tall, dark, perhaps somewhat heavily built.

That at least was not true.

The woman who had stood beside him at the altar was very much shorter than he had expected.

She must, he thought, have thrown back her veil when they had gone to the vestry to sign the register, but he had not looked at her simply because he had been afraid of what he might see.

When they had stood side by side receiving their guests there had been no time to do anything except shake hands, smile perfunctorily and accept with forced gratitude the congratulations that were repeated and repeated by each new-comer.

Perhaps the wine he had drunk at dinner was making him feel uncommonly stupid, Kelvin Ward thought.

Certainly he and Sir Anthony had consumed quite a considerable amount of brandy when they had eaten luncheon together at their Club.

Whatever the explanation was, Kelvin Ward felt he could not think clearly of what lay ahead.

All he knew was that he must do what was expected of him. He must behave conventionally.

If he did not do so, he had the ridiculous notion that his father-in-law would take him to task for it the following morning.

Had not Sir Erasmus already visualised the number of children they would have and set aside a Trust-Fund for them? He had tied up the future as neatly as he had tied up the present.

"Curse him to Hell!" Kelvin Ward muttered beneath his breath and then was ashamed of himself.

He seldom swore, knowing that in the Army it was a man's common and unbridled manner of expressing his feelings, but for his part he believed it only showed a lack of self-control.

Almost as if he were on parade, he called himself to attention and ordered himself to perform his duty.

He was married and he had been paid handsomely for giving his name and presumably his protection to the woman who was now his wife.

Whatever she was like, he would treat her with courtesy and consideration. But he would be master in his own household and his wife would obey him.

He put on a long robe of blue silk which Sir Anthony had insisted on his buying along with a number of shirts and other accessories at an expensive shop in St. James's.

"I have no need of anything new," Kelvin Ward had protested.

"What you do possess you have worn for far too long," Sir Anthony had answered, "and what is more, if you do not buy some decent clothes, I am certain your future father-in-law will buy them for you!"

It was this possibility which made Kelvin Ward acquiesce in his friend's suggestion. In fact, the long silk robe which almost touched the floor was very much more appropriate to the occasion than the garment he had worn for several years in the heat of India.

He caught a glimpse of himself in a mirror and saw a frown between his eyes; that his chin was set square in the manner that those who had served under him knew only too well meant that he was at his most authoritative.

He pulled open the door of his bed-room and walked across the flower-filled boudoir to the door on the other side of it.

Just for a moment he paused, thinking that Seraphina might be asleep and would not welcome his intrusion at this late hour.

Then he told himself savagely the sooner they both faced up to the situation the better, and knocking perfunctorily he opened the door.

The large room was lit only by a single candelabrum standing beside the bed. This was draped with velvet curtains hanging from a carved canopy which was reminiscent of a Pope's throne.

It was a big bed, high off the ground, with a white ermine cover and sheets and pillow-case deeply edged with fine Venetian lace.

Sitting upright was a very small figure, seeming dwarfed in the great bed.

For a moment Kelvin Ward thought he had made a mistake and come to the wrong room.

Then as he advanced nearer to the bed he saw that far from being the dark-haired, rather heavily built bride he had expected, there was a fairy-like creature who appeared to be little more than a child.

She had two enormous eyes in a very small face haloed by hair so fair that it was paler than the first rays of the rising sun.

She was staring at him with an expression of fear that he had thought never to see on a woman's face!

Kelvin Ward stopped beside the bed.

He could see that his bride was trembling and that her fingers, thin and delicate, were locked together so desperately that the knuckles showed white.

They looked at each other for a moment and then almost incredulously Kelvin Ward asked:

"Are you frightened of—me, Seraphina?"

There was a pause and then in a small breathless little voice he could hardly hear, she faltered:

"Y . . . you are so . . . big and . . . scowly!"

For the first time that day Kelvin Ward smiled.

"I cannot help being big, but I will try not to scowl!"

Seraphina's fingers twisted convulsively as she said a little above a whisper:

"C . . . could I . . . speak to you?"

"But of course," Kelvin Ward replied. "We have had no opportunity of talking to each other until now."

As he spoke he sat down on the edge of the bed facing her.

He saw a sudden tremor go through Seraphina.

For a moment she seemed to wince away from him and press herself against the pillows.

"I am listening," Kelvin Ward said gently, in what he hoped was a reassuring tone, "to what you want to tell me."

Seraphina's cheeks were as white as the pillows and her eyes were very dark and frightened.

"I . . . I wanted . . . to tell . . . you that . . . I am a . . . coward."

"A coward?" Kelvin Ward repeated in surprise.

"I cannot . . . help it. I . . . I do try and try to be . . . courageous . . . but all the time . . . I am . . . afraid."

"Suppose you tell me what has frightened you?" Kelvin Ward suggested.

She did not answer and he saw that she was fighting to find words. At length she whispered:

"You will ... think me very ... ignorant, but I know ... that when a ... man and a ... woman are married ... they do ... something together, but no-one has told me ... what it is."

She paused for a moment and then even more breathlessly, her words falling over themselves, she went on:

"If ... if you could please ... tell me what you are ... going to d-do before you ... do it ... I will try ... to be ... b-brave."

She was trembling now even more than before, and after a moment of almost incredulous surprise Kelvin Ward said:

"Are you telling me, Seraphina, that no-one talked to you about being married?"

"There was ... no-one with whom I could ... discuss it," she answered. "Miss Colville ... that was my Governess ... would never speak ... of such ... matters ... and I ... could not ask ... the servants."

"No, of course not," Kelvin Ward agreed.

There was silence for a moment and then he said:

"Did you want to marry me, Seraphina?"

"No! I could not ... believe that I ... had to ... I ... I could not think I must ... do such a thing when Papa ... first told me."

"You informed him you had no wish to be married?"

"Papa ... would not ... listen! When he gives an ... order, he expects it ... to be obeyed."

There was a faint twist to Kelvin Ward's lips as he acknowledged the truth of this.

"Did your father tell you why you were to marry me?"

Seraphina shook her head. Her fair hair gleamed for a moment in the light of the candles.

"Papa just said ... he had chosen my ... husband for me ... and I was to be ... married on ... Thursday. Just ... like that!"

"Why did you not plead with him to give you more time and suggest that we might meet each other first?"

"Papa never ... listens to me," Seraphina said. "I did think of ... running away ... but I had ... no-where to go."

Kelvin Ward did not speak. This was something he had never imagined could happen.

"Why did you ... want to ... marry ... me?" Seraphina asked after a moment.

Kelvin Ward chose his words carefully before replying:

"Like you, I had little choice in the matter."

"Papa ... made you?"

"Yes. Your father made me!"

"How could he do ... that?"

Kelvin Ward told her part of the truth.

"One reason was that I had no money, Seraphina, and you are a very rich young woman."

"You ... wanted my ... money?"

"I wanted a comparatively small sum for a business venture in India."

"And to ... get it you ... had to marry ... me."

"Yes."

"There was no ... other way ... for you to ... obtain it?"

"No."

There was a silence and he saw she was thinking over what he had told her.

"What was the ... other reason?" she questioned.

Kelvin Ward did not reply and she said nervously:

"Perhaps ... I should not ... have asked!"

"Why not?" he said. "It is best if there are no secrets between us. Your father had a certain hold over me."

"So he . . . forced you to . . . marry me."

"Yes."

"I . . . I am . . . sorry."

"For you or for me?" Kelvin Ward asked.

"I suppose . . . for both of us. I had thought of . . . marrying . . . sometime . . . but . . ."

Her voice died away.

"But you hoped you would fall in love."

She did not answer, but he thought he saw a little glint in her eyes and added:

"I am sure you dreamed of a Prince Charming who certainly did not scowl at you!"

"You do not look quite so . . . fierce now," she replied, "but I thought you were . . . angry in the Church, and I was . . . sure of it when we were receiving the guests."

"I am ashamed it was so obvious," Kelvin Ward apologised.

"I . . . I do not think anyone else would have known," Seraphina said seriously. "It is just that sometimes I am aware how . . . people are feeling . . . even when they try to disguise it."

"I can only express my regret that you too were forced into this marriage," Kelvin Ward said. "I suppose every girl wants to fall in love."

"And . . . and you?" Seraphina asked. "Did you not want to . . . be in love . . . before you made someone your . . . wife?"

"I had no wish to marry anyone," Kelvin Ward replied honestly. "At the same time, if I had to do so, I would obviously prefer to choose my bride myself."

"Papa has been very . . . dictatorial ever since . . . Mama died," Seraphina said. "She was the only person who could make him change his mind and be . . . kind and understanding."

She gave a little sigh.

"If I had refused to marry you . . . as I wanted to do . . . I think he would have . . . beaten me."

Kelvin Ward stiffened.

"Are you really telling me your father beats you?" he asked.

"Not since I was fifteen," Seraphina answered. "But after Mama's ... death, he often punished me not ... I think ... for anything wrong I had done but because he was angry with me for being ... alive when she was ... dead."

There was so much perception in this that Kelvin Ward thought that behind the child-like exterior Seraphina must have a good brain.

"And you believe that if you had opposed him now he would have offered you physical violence? It seems incredible!"

Even as he spoke he knew it was not incredible. Soldiers were flogged in the Army, boys were birched at school, the head of a household would whip not only his children but often his servants.

What really shocked him, Kelvin Ward admitted to himself, was that anyone should beat anything so vulnerable, so obviously acutely sensitive as Seraphina.

"Papa never allows ... anyone to oppose him," she answered, "and besides, I have told you I am a ... coward!"

"I think you are rather harsh on yourself."

"No, I am not! So many things ... frighten me. It is horrible being so fearful! It is a ... weakness that creeps up inside me. My heart ... flutters, my hands ... shake and I want to run away and hide."

"And yet you faced me," Kelvin Ward said gently.

"I was very ... frightened! I knew you would ... despise me, but now you are talking to me it is not nearly as ... bad as I had ... anticipated."

"I am glad about that!" he said with a smile, "but of course I am not Prince Charming. In fact I have an uncomfortable suspicion I am the wicked Demon!"

"I did not . . . say so," Seraphina answered.

"I am facing facts," Kelvin Ward said. "Now listen, Seraphina, I have a suggestion to make."

"What is . . . it?" she asked.

He saw the fear come back into her eyes.

He wanted to put his hand over hers reassuringly, then he told himself it might frighten her more.

"It is this," he said quietly. "Neither of us wished to get married, and I can quite understand your finding the idea strange and indeed frightening. I propose that we let the world think we are husband and wife, which indeed we are, but when we are alone together as we are now, let us try to get to know each other. Perhaps we could be friends."

"You mean . . . you . . . you will not . . . sleep here with me . . . tonight?" Seraphina faltered.

Kelvin Ward shook his head.

"I will only sleep with you when you ask me to," he answered. "As I have said, we must get to know each other, and perhaps to like what we find, before we begin to talk about love."

"Suppose we . . . never . . . love each other?" Seraphina asked in a low voice.

"I think we must cross that bridge when we come to it," Kelvin Ward replied. "At the moment I know nothing about you and you know nothing about me. We have quite a lot to discover about each other."

"Can we . . . really do . . . that?"

"It will be our secret," Kelvin Ward said, "something nobody else need know about. To the world we will just be an ordinary married couple."

And as he spoke he longed to add: 'and that includes your father too.'

He had the feeling that he was scoring off Sir Erasmus in coming to an arrangement with Seraphina. He must have seen how sensitive his daughter was.

How could he have pitch-forked the girl into marriage with no preparation for what she would have to encounter, with no idea of what a bridegroom would expect of his bride?

He wondered if in actual fact Sir Erasmus was unaware that his daughter had not been enlightened about the facts of marriage.

Then he was sure that even if he had known she was so innocent it would have made no difference. Seraphina was, like her husband, just a part of his plan!

Aloud Kelvin Ward said:

"Then we have made a pact, Seraphina, and may I say I shall look forward to getting to know you better."

"A pact!" she repeated.

"Shall we shake hands on it?"

He held out his hand as he spoke. For a moment Seraphina hesitated and then she laid her fingers in his palm.

They were very cold and he felt them quiver almost like a small bird that had been caught in a net.

He would have liked to raise them to his lips, but then he thought she might misunderstand his action.

He released her and rose to his feet.

"Good-night, Seraphina," he said. "Try to sleep. Tomorrow we set off from Tilbury for a new world. It will be a voyage of discovery. There will be many new places for you to see and enjoy."

He paused. Her eyes were on his and he saw a gleam of excitement in them.

"I promise you as far as I am concerned there will be nothing to frighten you," he finished.

"Thank you," Seraphina said in her breathless little voice. "Thank you . . . very much."

Chapter Three

As the S.S. *Tiberius* reached the western end
of the English Channel and turned to cross the Bay
of Biscay, Kelvin Ward thought with a feeling of
satisfaction that he had left behind not only England but his father-in-law in particular.

He had almost counted the minutes from the
morning after their wedding to the moment when
he could say good-bye to Sir Erasmus.

They had taken a train to Tilbury and Sir
Erasmus, arriving at Malton House after breakfast,
had accompanied them.

It had not been such an embarrassing journey
as Kelvin Ward had anticipated because Sir Anthony Fanshawe had also come to see them off.

"I consider it my duty to you as your Best
Man," he had said firmly.

Kelvin Ward had the suspicion that Sir Erasmus did not welcome his company but there was
nothing he could do but make the best of it.

They had travelled in considerable style in a
special coach reserved for the party which consisted of themselves and a number of servants—quite

an unnecessary amount, Kelvin Ward thought—to
see them off.

Only Seraphina's personal maid was actually
to go with them to India.

Sir Erasmus had suggested that Kelvin Ward
should take a valet, but on this point his son-in-law
had been unexpectedly firm.

"I shall have an Indian servant in India," he
said, "and I should not be surprised if Seraphina's
maid is not home-sick almost as soon as she steps
onto dry land and wishes to return."

On this point Sir Erasmus conceded defeat,
but in other matters he was adamant that they
should embark in style.

Kelvin Ward realised when for the first time
he saw his wife and her father together that Seraphina seemed crushed by Sir Erasmus into a quiet,
submissive figure with no will of her own.

Nevertheless he could not help appreciating
the fact that she was indeed very lovely.

She was taller than he had expected to find her
after he had seen the child-like figure in the bed.
The impression she gave of fragility was due in
part to the fact that she was slim with very fine
bones.

What is more, she moved with a grace which
made every other woman seem clumsy and somehow cumbersome in comparison.

Her eyes, which were unexpectedly the deep
blue of a Summer sea, had sought his a little shyly
when they had met at breakfast.

It was not laid in the vast Dining-Room that
had been used for the wedding-reception, but in a
small Morning-Room where they were however
waited on by the Butler and three footmen.

There was an overwhelming choice of food
served on silver dishes which were far too dazzling
for so early in the morning.

Kelvin Ward made a private note that if this
was the sort of opulence Seraphina would expect in

the houses they would occupy either in India or in England she would be disappointed.

Then he told himself this display was none of her choosing.

He was glad to leave Malton House; the enormous rooms, the expensive furnishings, the valuable furniture and superlative pictures might be an appropriate background for Sir Erasmus, but they made Kelvin Ward feel he had eaten a surfeit of *pâté de foie gras*.

Travelling to Tilbury in their comfortable private coach, Sir Erasmus talked of the best method of travelling.

"Always go to the top," he said. "I, personally, get Thomas Cook himself to arrange my journeys. You should do the same."

Kelvin Ward was amused at the thought that the great Cook would be personally concerned with lesser fry.

Thomas Cook was 'the booking clerk' of the Empire and could arrange transport to any land anywhere in the world on which an Englishman might wish to set foot.

His brown mahogany offices, with whirling air-cooling fans and brass teller's cages, were to be found in every Imperial city.

Cook's held the concession for operating steamers on the River Nile. Cook's provided donkeys, boats and carriages. Cook's organised trips to Constantinople, Australia, or pilgrimages to Mecca.

There were porters, waiters, couriers, gharri-drivers, fly-whisked dragonmen, Chinamen in Malaya and bearded Sikhs, all wearing Cook's familiar embroidered jerseys.

"I remember Cook's arranging a visit to Europe for an Indian Prince," Kelvin Ward said. "His entourage included two hundred servants, twenty Chefs, thirty-three tigers, ten elephants, a thousand packing-cases and a howitzer."

Sir Erasmus changed the subject.

Seraphina hardly spoke. It was only when they reached Tilbury that Kelvin Ward learnt that she had a sense of humour.

The Station-Master in his top-hat and covered with an immense amount of gold-braid escorted them with much pomp and ceremony from the Station to the dockside where he handed them over to officials from the S.S. *Tiberius*.

A slow-speaking solemn man, he said as he left them:

"I can only pray, Sir and Madam, that Almighty God dispatches you in safety to your destination."

"Just as if we were parcels!" Seraphina said in a soft voice which only Kelvin Ward could hear.

He met her eyes, found there was a twinkle in them and realised she was not as crushed or submissive as she appeared.

"Good-bye, my dear," Sir Erasmus said to his daughter when it was time for visitors to go ashore. "Write to me and I shall be kept informed as to your well-being."

Kelvin Ward wondered if this was a threat or a warning, but Sir Erasmus's handshake was warm and he said genially:

"Good-bye, my boy—I expect great things of you."

It was Sir Anthony who made everything seem normal with the words:

"Off to the sunshine in style and with the prettiest companion any man could desire—you are a lucky dog, Kelvin!"

With a small bonnet on her hair and tied under her chin with blue ribbons which matched her eyes, Seraphina did look very lovely.

She did not appear distressed at leaving her father and after he and Sir Anthony had gone ashore, she waved to them from the top deck as the ship pulled away from the Quayside.

Then because it was cold and there was a

heavy drizzle Kelvin Ward persuaded her to seek the warmth of their cabin.

The Bridal Suite was quite impressive, but in the Sitting-Room filled with bouquets of hot-house flowers, baskets of fruit, boxes of chocolates, rugs and cushions, besides their own personal belongings, there was hardly room to move.

There were two State-Rooms, Kelvin Ward noted with satisfaction, and a small adjacent cabin where Seraphina's maid would sleep.

It was in all considerably different from the accommodation he had been allotted in Troop-Ships or the small uncomfortable cabin he had occupied in the Steamer in which he had returned from India because it was cheap.

He had in fact never before travelled in one of the very latest ships which, despite their luxurious interior, were ugly, square-prowed vessels with two slightly leaning funnels beside four tall masts and their complicated rigging.

The Steam-Ship lines were intensely proud of their new ships and had begun to advertise them extravagantly.

The engines of the S.S. *Tiberius*, Kelvin Ward had read, were so smooth it was sometimes difficult to believe they were operating at all.

He was also informed that "the third-class arrangements are particularly complete." The object was, so the advertisement said, "to ensure the comfort of the steerage passengers and to avoid any annoyance to the travellers in the first and second Saloons."

Kelvin Ward found a similar brochure to the one he had read amongst the flowers and fruit on the table in the centre of the cabin.

Because he felt the first moments when he and Seraphina were alone might be awkward he picked it up and said:

"This attempts to tell us how fortunate we are to be on the *Tiberius*! You will be interested to know there is an organ in the picture gallery, and in each first-class cabin there is 'an arrangement by which the electric lighting can be turned on or off at pleasure by the occupant.' "

Seraphina laughed.

"It must be fun for those who have never seen electric light before."

She took off her heavy travelling cloak which was trimmed with Russian sable.

Kelvin Ward saw she was wearing an attractive gown of sapphire wool trimmed with satin against which her hair appeared so fair that he found himself thinking of the first primroses of Spring.

Seraphina looked round the cabin.

"Do you think we could move some of these things?" she asked. "Papa has overwhelmed us with comforts which I am sure we will never want."

"I will summon a steward and we will dispose of them," Kelvin Ward said with a smile.

"And I think there are really too many ... flowers."

She gave him a little nervous glance as if she expected him to disagree with her.

"We will ask if there is anyone on board who might appreciate some of them," he answered, "and I am quite sure we would never be able to eat such an enormous amount of fruit!"

He thought that Seraphina looked at him gratefully. When he had given the order and had gone away to explore the ship, he came back to find her sitting at a table sorting out her books.

She had brought almost a Library with her and he was interested to see that most of them were about India.

"You certainly intend to be well informed before we arrive," he remarked.

"I do not want to become a nuisance by asking you too many questions."

"I am greatly looking forward to showing you

the country where I have spent so many years in
the Army," Kelvin Ward said.

He found—what he had not expected—that
she appeared perfectly content to sit reading and
often when- he was with her not to expect constant
conversation.

He had in fact never known a woman, he told
himself, who could be so restful.

Then in all honesty he had to confess he had
not often been alone with a woman for any length
of time except when he was flirting or making love
to her.

The *Tiberius* was expected to take twenty
days on the journey to Bombay. After the first
night at sea they found they had left England well
behind and were steaming South into the Bay of
Biscay.

A fog, which had made the first hours of their
journey rather unpleasant, lifted and the foghorn
had ceased to blare out noisily every few minutes.

There was however, Kelvin Ward noticed, a
heavy swell and he guessed from the fact that the
sails were being taken in that there was a chance of
encountering rough waters in the Bay.

However he did not wish to anticipate trouble
and hoped that Seraphina was as good a sailor as
he was himself.

They went down to luncheon in the first-class
Dining-Saloon where, surrounded by potted palms,
they were waited upon by bearded stewards.

Kelvin Ward, who had already inspected the
whole of the ship, found that in the second-class
Saloon the passengers sat at long communal tables
with decanters slung on trays from the ceiling above
their heads.

He also discovered that passengers were advised to bring deck-chairs with them, plainly
marked with the owner's name.

Needless to say, he learnt that Sir Erasmus

had known of this and provided for them no less than six chairs in case, Kelvin Ward supposed, they should wish to converse with people who joined them from other parts of the ship.

He went back to the Sitting-Room to find Seraphina reading.

A steward had spoken to him before he had gone on deck and he said as he entered:

"There appears to be a complaint that we are taking up more than our fair share of the corridor outside our cabins. I could hardly imagine one small person would need such a multitudinous amount of luggage."

"There does seem to be rather a lot," Seraphina agreed.

"The steward was enquiring whether it would be possible for some of the trunks to be put in the hold, unless you need them on the voyage."

"I am sure they can all go," Seraphina answered. "I believe they contain only gowns that are suitable for India."

Kelvin Ward looked surprised.

"How could you have bought so large a trousseau in so short a time?"

"Papa ordered them," Seraphina answered. "Martha told me that they had arrived at Malton House long before we came up from the country."

Kelvin Ward felt a sudden surge of anger.

Sir Erasmus had been so certain that he must accept his proposition that he had ordered Seraphina's trousseau before they had even discussed it!

Once again Kelvin Ward had the feeling he was caught in a trap, that he was being manipulated and there was nothing he could do about it.

Suddenly he heard a nervous little voice ask:

"What . . . have I . . . said to make you . . . angry?"

"What makes you think I am angry?" he enquired.

"You . . . you are . . . scowling."

With an effort Kelvin Ward forced the frown from between his eyes.

"I am sorry," he said, "but I am surprised that you should be content to let your father choose your clothes for you."

"He did not actually choose them," Seraphina answered. "He orders them from Madame Marietta, who always dressed Mama and who knows the colours and materials I like."

"I see . . ." Kelvin Ward remarked.

Although he told himself it was foolish, he felt somehow relieved that he would not feel every time he saw his wife in a particularly attractive gown that it had been her father's choice.

As Kelvin Ward had suspected, the sea grew steadily worse.

By four o'clock in the afternoon the wind had assumed almost gale force, the ship was pitching and tossing and the waves were breaking over the bow.

At the same time the sun had come out and there was something majestic and very beautiful in the emerald-green water with its frothing silver spray.

Kelvin Ward went on deck and stood for a long time watching the sea, feeling something primitive in him glorying in the roughness and violence of it.

Then he remembered Seraphina and wondered if she had succumbed, as he was quite certain the majority of women on board had done, to sea-sickness.

He went back to the cabin, seeing on the way stewards scuttling along the corridors with basins and towels, and knew there would be few people in the Dining-Saloon that night.

He opened the door of their Sitting-Room to find Seraphina sitting in a corner of the sofa.

She did not speak nor did she appear to be

suffering from *mal de mer*, but when he looked at
her Kelvin Ward knew she was frightened.

"Are you all right, Seraphina?" he asked.

She raised her face to his and he saw the fear
which made her pupils dilate and her eyes seem
dark.

"Are we ... going to the ... bottom?" she
asked in a very small voice.

He crossed the cabin and seated himself beside
her.

"No, of course not," he said reassuringly,
"there is no danger."

"I ... I have read ... about ship-wrecks at ...
sea," Seraphina said, "and there were a ... great
many of them ... last year."

"Not with ships of this size! I promise you,
Seraphina, we are not going to founder or turn tur-
tle, or suffer any of the horrifying accidents you
have read about in the newspapers."

"I ... I cannot ... help being ... frightened,"
she said after a moment.

"I understand," he answered reassuringly. "It
is a very nasty feeling and that is why I want you
to do something for me."

"What is ... that?" Seraphina asked.

"I want you to come with me up on deck and
watch the waves breaking against the bow. It is a
very impressive sight, and I assure you it is far less
alarming when one is out in the open than sitting
cooped up in here."

She seemed to hesitate and he said with a
smile which women had always found irresistible:

"Trust me. I promise that you will not be
swept over-board!"

"I will . . . come if you . . . want me to,"
Seraphina agreed.

He went into her State-Room to find her
travelling cloak.

There was no sign of her maid and he was

quite certain that Martha was prostrate with sea-sickness.

He opened the cupboard door and noticed a sweet fresh fragrance which came from Seraphina's clothes.

It reminded him of Spring flowers, and he smelt it again as Seraphina holding his arm went with him on deck.

Patches of sky interspersed between the clouds were vividly blue and the sun gave the sea strange mysterious depths as the waves rose and fell and showered their spray with what was almost like the sound of music against the sturdy prow.

Kelvin Ward was aware that Seraphina was clinging to his arm with both hands in what was an almost convulsive grip.

Then as they stood sheltered against the super-structure, he felt her gradually relax. Looking down at her he saw a child-like delight replace the fear on her face.

"You are right!" she said at length. "It is majestic!"

"I hoped you would think so," Kelvin Ward smiled.

It was difficult to talk against the wind and, after they had stood almost in silence a quarter of an hour, he took her back to the State-Room.

"Thank you," she said as he helped her out of her cloak. "I am ashamed of having been so foolish."

"It is the unknown that is frightening," Kelvin Ward replied. "Now that you have seen the sea and know why it is making the ship move in this somewhat uncomfortable fashion, there is nothing to fear."

"No, of course not," Seraphina said, "but no-one has ever . . . explained things to me before."

"What about your Tutors and Governesses?" he asked. "Your father told me you had been intensively educated."

"I have been over-educated!"

"What do you mean by that?"

"I have been stuffed with knowledge ever since I can remember," Seraphina said, "But I have never been allowed to think for myself."

"And do you want to?" Kelvin Ward asked.

"I try to," she replied. "But every time I had an idea which I thought original, I was always told crushingly that Darwin, or Dr. Johnson, or Socrates had thought of it before me, and I had much better quote what they said than try to express my own mind."

"That must have been very frustrating," he agreed.

"I suppose because after Mama's death I have had no-one to talk to about the things I felt and the things I imagine," Seraphina went on, "I have become so . . . unsure of myself."

Kelvin Ward wished to say that he well knew there could be no chance of her being herself or sure of anything in her father's presence, but instead he said gently:

"I hope now you will always tell me what you think, because I promise you I am very interested."

"Are you really?" Seraphina asked, "or are you just saying that because you . . . feel you . . . ought to?"

"I am really interested," Kelvin Ward replied, "and I hope you will be interested in anything I tell you."

"I am! I want you to tell me everything!" Seraphina said eagerly. "Friends share their joys and their sorrows, do they not?"

"They do indeed!"

He saw the smile of gratitude she gave him, which seemed to illuminate her small face.

She was like a foal, he told himself, that would shy away at the expectation of being bridled, but could be coaxed by kindness into trusting the hand that wished to touch it.

It seemed incredible that Sir Erasmus should have fathered anything so utterly alien to his character and over-positive personality, but it was obvious that Seraphina must resemble her mother.

The storm brought them a certain amount of discomfort and, as Kelvin Ward had expected, there were few people in the Dining-Saloon either for luncheon or dinner during the next two days.

When they reached Gibraltar and passed into the Mediterranean the sea was comparatively calm and over-head there was a sky blue as a Madonna's robe.

They stopped at Gibraltar only for a few hours and there was no time to go ashore.

At Malta, too, as they were behind schedule owing to the storm, the passengers were not permitted to leave the ship.

Malta was one of the main posts of the submarine cable.

The British had encompassed their Empire with cables and in the last ten years had developed a wholly British world-embracing system.

Morse keys clicked across the oceans and miraculously linked all the Continents with one another.

At Malta cable-messages were brought aboard and Kelvin Ward walked into the cabin with four in his hands.

One was addressed to Seraphina, which he gave to her. The others were his and he opened them one by one.

The first was from Sir Anthony sending them his good wishes, another was from his business friends in Bombay.

Kelvin Ward had cabled them that he not only had the money to invest in the scheme they had envisaged but also was prepared to make his share five times greater than the five thousand pounds they had originally considered necessary.

Their reply, despite being economically worded, was ecstatic with delight.

Kelvin Ward opened another communication. It was from Sir Erasmus:

> Have bought on your behalf two ships of five thousand tons and instructed them to proceed Bombay. Have notified your Company to receive them.
>
> Erasmus Malton

Kelvin Ward, having read the cable, made a savage ejaculation of anger and in a sudden fury crumpled it up in the palm of his hand.

He had forgotten that Seraphina was in the cabin with him until he heard her voice say:

"What has ... upset you?"

He did not trust his voice to answer and she went on:

"Surely I have a right ... to know ..."

"Of course you have a right," Kelvin Ward interposed, his voice hard and harsh. "You have the right because this is *your* money that I am expending. *Your* money which had bought me and which makes it impossible for me to arrange or direct anything for myself. But make no mistake, one day I will pay you back—every penny. And when that happens, I shall be my own master!"

As he finished speaking he stood, his breath coming quickly, looking down at the crumpled ball he had made of the telegram.

Then, because he was ashamed of himself for allowing his rage to get the upper hand, he slowly opened up the cable again.

He attempted to smooth the creases from it and laid it with the other two cables he had received on the desk in front of him.

He took a deep breath and with an effort turned round.

"I must explain, Seraphina . . ." he began, only to find that he was alone in the cabin.

He realised then how angry his voice must have sounded. It had been wrong and almost unforgivable to take out on her his rage against Sir Erasmus.

At the same time he could hardly bear to think that his own project, one he wished to develop with his friends in his own way, was being interfered with by his father-in-law.

Again he told himself it was not Seraphina's fault.

She could not be held responsible and he must try not to make her suffer for any action of her father's.

He walked across to her bed-room door, knocked, and when she did not answer he walked in.

She was sitting on the side of the bed and as he entered she rose hastily to her feet to stand at the port-hole with her back to him.

He guessed that she was trying to hide her tears.

He shut the door behind him and came a little nearer.

"I interrupted you in the middle of a sentence, Seraphina," he said gently. "Will you finish what you were going to say?"

There was a long silence and he knew she was fighting to control her voice. Then in a tremulous tone she said:

"I . . . I was . . . only going to . . . say that I have a . . . right . . . as your . . . friend to share . . . your . . . problems."

"I thought too late that was what you had been about to tell me," Kelvin Ward answered. "Please forgive me, Seraphina, I should not have spoken as I did."

"Does ... money matter so ... much?" she asked unexpectedly.

"It matters a great deal when you do not possess any," he answered. "But between friends there should be more important things."

She did not answer and after a moment he said pleadingly:

"Please turn round and talk to me, Seraphina. I am very contrite."

She wiped her eyes and turned.

Her face was very pale and her eye-lashes were still wet with the tears she had shed.

Kelvin Ward could not help thinking she was one of the few women he had ever seen who could cry and still look attractive.

She looked at him nervously. He sat down on the side of the bed and held out his hand.

"Come and sit down," he suggested, "Otherwise I shall think you are still angry with me."

She gave him a watery little smile.

"*You* were ... angry!" she corrected. "Was it ... Papa who upset you?"

"Yes, it was your father."

He told her about the two ships and showed her the cable.

She read it carefully and then she said:

"I know you are thinking that Papa is ... interfering and trying in a way to ... show his ... power over you. But that is not quite ... true."

"Then what is?" Kelvin Ward asked.

"Mama said once," Seraphina answered, "that everyone has to have ... someone or something in their lives to ... love."

Kelvin Ward looked at her quizzically.

"Go on."

"When Mama was alive ... Papa loved her, and I think looking back that everything in which he was successful was a kind of ... triumph because he could ... show off to Mama how ... clever he was."

"I can understand that," Kelvin Ward said in his deep voice.

"Then when Mama . . . died," Seraphina went on, "the love he had felt for her was transferred into what he was . . . doing. He now loves what Mama used to call his . . . 'plots and plans.' "

"That is a good name for them."

"It is not just that they bring in . . . money," Seraphina said, "it is because he is creating . . . something."

"An Empire of his own," Kelvin Ward said with a twist to his lips.

"Have you ever seen a man working on a carpet?" Seraphina asked. "I mean those that are hand-made?"

"Yes, I suppose I have—in Persia," Kelvin Ward answered, surprised at the turn in the conversation.

"Then you know that he works at the back of it. It just looks a jumble of stitches. Then when he turns the carpet over there is a beautiful, intricate, perfect pattern."

Kelvin Ward looked at her appreciatively.

"I understand what you are trying to say about your father, but it is hard for an outsider like myself not to suspect his motives."

"It took me a little time to understand them too," Seraphina admitted. "I used to want him to love me because I was so lonely after Mama died. Then I realised I was not nearly so exciting as setting up a new company in Canada, or . . . buying two ships for . . . you in Bombay. "

Kelvin Ward was silent for a moment and then he said:

"You are a very remarkable person, Seraphina. It is beginning to astonish me how much wisdom you have in that small head of yours."

"I am not really wise," Seraphina said. "In fact you know how . . . foolish I am."

"I think that is the last adjective I would apply to you," Kelvin Ward smiled. "And when I am angry I will try to remember your explanation of your father's actions."

The next day Seraphina's perception surprised him yet again.

He was glad to see that she had made a few acquaintances on board.

Kelvin Ward was well aware that they were an outstanding couple, and because their wedding had been reported in the newspapers and Seraphina's fortune would have lost nothing in the telling, they aroused a great deal of curiosity and speculation amongst the other passengers.

People made every effort to talk to them, and though Seraphina was shy, her good manners and natural courtesy could not allow her to be anything but polite and charming to those who approached them.

Coming into the cabin after taking exercise on deck, Kelvin Ward was aware immediately that something had perturbed Seraphina.

He had grown to recognise the different expressions on her face—in fact he had never known that a woman's face could be as expressive as Seraphina's.

He found too that when she was frightened or when she was happy there was an aura about her that was inescapable.

So without any preliminaries he asked:

"What has upset you?"

She did not answer for a moment, then she replied:

"You did not tell me that one day you will be a . . . Duke!"

Kelvin Ward was surprised.

"I thought your father would have told you."

"Nobody told me," she answered.

"How do you know now?"

"One of the . . . ladies asked me if I would like

to borrow her magazine. I looked at the pictures of
the Opening of Parliament and she said:

" 'It must be exciting for you, Mrs Ward, to
think that one day you will take your place
amongst those glittering Peeresses.'

"I looked at her in surprise and she went on:

" 'I mean of course when your husband be-
comes the Duke of Uxbridge.' "

Kelvin Ward sat down on the chair opposite
Seraphina.

"Why does the idea perturb you?"

"I . . . I would not . . . know how to . . . behave
as a . . . Duchess," Seraphina replied. "It would
mean that you . . . would be very . . . important
and I should have to . . . entertain. And . . . anyway
I am . . . too small to wear . . . a tiara."

"You wore one on your wedding-day," Kelvin
Ward reminded her.

"Papa . . . made me. I thought it was over-
powering because it was . . . so big and rather . . .
vulgar."

Kelvin Ward had thought the same thing himself and he said with a smile:

"Very well then. When you become a Duchess
we will dispense with the tiara—or find a very
small one!"

"You are laughing at me!" Seraphina said ac-
cusingly.

"I cannot allow you to upset yourself about
something that may not happen for at least fifteen
years, or longer," Kelvin Ward said. "Besides, not·
all Dukes parade their importance socially. My
Uncle certainly does not."

"Why not?" Seraphina enquired.

"Because he is a miserable miser who would
no more spend money on a tiara than fly over the
moon!"

"A miser?" Seraphina questioned.

"He begrudges every expense. He would not

lend me the money I needed for my shipping project in Bombay."

"He refused you?"

"Yes, he refused me, just as he refused to help my mother when she was dying and had to have several operations."

Kelvin Ward was silent for a moment and then he said:

"He is deformed in body and mind. He is the meanest and most disliked man in England. There is nothing about him which is commendable."

He could not conceal the note of bitterness and hatred in his voice and after a moment Seraphina said softly:

"You should not allow other people to affect you ... emotionally, as your Uncle and my Papa do."

He looked at her enquiringly and she went on:

"Mama always said to be hurt physically is horrible but nothing was worse than mental injuries. That which wounds our hearts and our minds leaves scars."

"You think your father and my Uncle do that to me?" Kelvin Ward asked.

"Hatred is something which turns against ourselves," Seraphina said. "When you are hating them the emotion poisons ... you."

Kelvin Ward stared at her in astonishment, and then she said nervously:

"Please ... I—I am not trying to ... lecture you, but you did say I could ... tell you ... what I thought."

"I want to hear your thoughts and understand them," Kelvin Ward said. "You are full of surprises, Seraphina."

"I think perhaps your Uncle, like Papa, has to have something to love, so he loves money. For a miser, I have always been told, to save a shilling is as exciting as for another man to climb a mountain—or win the hand of the woman he loves."

"You have given me a lot to think about," Kelvin Ward said simply. "Thank you, Seraphina. I must try not to hate and I know you will help me."

"Just as you will ... help me not to be ... afraid."

"And you have forgiven me for my unkindness yesterday, when I vented my anger against your father on you?"

"There is nothing to ... forgive," she replied. "It was foolish of me to be upset."

"You had every justification," he said. "I was very ashamed of myself."

He smiled beguilingly and added:

"And that is an emotion in which I have not often indulged."

"Humility is, I believe, good for the soul," she said, and her eyes were twinkling.

"As I have already remarked," Kelvin Ward replied, "you are full of surprises, Seraphina."

Later that evening Kelvin Ward found himself talking with Seraphina in a way that he could never remember talking with a woman before.

Always when he had dined alone with one there had been the quick, witty repartee of sophistication; the intimate glances which meant more than their lips were saying; the tingling awareness that this was just the prelude to a different type of closeness.

The women who had been in Kelvin Ward's life had all been beautiful in their own way and some of them had been intelligent.

The latter were in the minority because intelligent women were few and far between.

But there were those with whom he had discussed politics or the details of Regimental life and found them willing listeners.

Seraphina was different.

He could never remember before having talked about the fundamental issues of human life with a female.

Women, if they had souls, usually did not wish to speak about them. They were far more interested in their hearts—or rather his heart—where it concerned them.

Men, on the other hand, usually found it slightly embarrassing to discuss anything but material facts.

There had, however, been men in India with whom Kelvin Ward had talked about the spiritual and mystical aspects of religion because to the Indians it was an inescapable part of their everyday life.

He had too in the course of his travels about the country met Saddhus, Fakirs and Yogis. Men who were animated, elevated and inspired by their faith.

They had aroused in Kelvin Ward a curiosity and interest that was perhaps unusual in an Englishman.

But he had never thought to talk with a woman about the vague stirrings of spirituality within him; of the things which made him feel that he wished to know more than lay on the surface of life, and to dig deeper into his own subconscious awareness of the world behind the world.

Least of all did he imagine for one moment he would exchange opinions on such abstruse matters with his bride—a girl of eighteen!

Dressed in a cloud of pale green tulle which made her look lovely but very young, Seraphina to his astonishment was saying, her soft voice very serious:

"What I am sure is important is not so much what people do as the motive behind their action."

"Explain what you mean by that."

"I have always felt," Seraphina answered slowly, "that to hang a man for murder is wrong unless we can discover the fundamental reason, which he may not know himself, why he committed the crime."

She looked at Kelvin Ward to see if he understood and went on:

"The same applies in other things. For instance, when you were speaking about your Uncle being a miser, I thought afterwards that because he is a deformed and unhappy person he is trying to find something stable, solid and valuable as compensation for the way he looks and feels.

"I have never thought of that," Kelvin Ward said quietly.

"I suppose we should all have an entirely different judgment of the human beings round us if we looked behind the obvious," Seraphina continued. "I used to try to work out why the people in our household and in the village behaved the way they did."

She paused to add shyly:

"I know very little about . . . life and perhaps you will . . . laugh at me, but I can not help feeling that wherever they live, however rich or poor they are, everyone is more or less motivated by the same impulses."

"Of course they are," Kelvin Ward said, "and our impulses are usually stronger than our willpower. They are why we must learn self-control."

"Yes, of course," Seraphina agreed.

"Discipline is something most people dislike," Kelvin Ward said, "and yet without discipline both outward and inward we cannot be civilised."

Seraphina thought that over and she said:

"In the Army you have a lot of discipline. Is it effective?"

"It is essential," Kelvin Ward answered. "A man who is going into battle must learn to obey orders. Without such discipline he would have little chance of survival."

Then he added:

"A good Regiment depends on its discipline and *'esprit de corps.'* "

Seraphina did not answer but he saw her looking at him speculatively and he asked:

"What are you thinking?"

"I was thinking," she said, "that when I told you everyone had to have something to ... love, I know what matters most to you."

"What is it?" Kelvin Ward enquired.

"Your Regiment."

"How can you know that?"

"Your voice changes when you speak about it. You love it and I think now it was not only having to marry me which made you so angry, but also because you had to leave your real love ... which was more important to you than anything else."

"I am frightened of you, Seraphina," Kelvin Ward said. "You are too perceptive. If I wanted to hide anything from you, it might be difficult."

"I hope you will not want to do that," Seraphina said.

Then to Kelvin Ward's surprise the colour rose in her cheeks.

He waited and after a moment she murmured:

"Yet ... perhaps ... there are things ... which you would not ... wish me to know."

"If there are I have no idea what they could be," he answered.

He was about to ask what she had in mind when a waiter at his elbow interrupted to ask if he required anything.

This made him realise that the Dining-Saloon had emptied and they were the last people still sitting at table.

"Let us go upstairs," he suggested to Seraphina.

He rose as he spoke, to place her wrap over her shoulders and she moved gracefully ahead of him.

The soft fullness of her green tulle bustle floated behind her like the wake left in the track of a ship.

Chapter Four

Seraphina and Kelvin Ward reached the top of the stairway.

"Would you prefer to have coffee in the Saloon or in our cabin?" he asked.

Then before Seraphina could reply a woman came towards them.

She was a striking figure and her beauty was accentuated by the exceedingly décolleté and elaborate black gown she wore.

The darkness of it was a vivid contrast to the whiteness of her skin and to the pearls and diamonds which encircled her neck and glittered in her ears.

"Kelvin!"

She held out both her hands impulsively and moved forward with a rustle of skirts and a provocative smile on her lips.

"I heard you were on board, Auriel," Kelvin Ward replied. "May I introduce my wife? Seraphina, this is Lady Braithwaite."

"How delightful to meet you! It would have happened sooner had I not been *hors de combat* during that terrible storm," Lady Braithwaite explained. "Your husband knows what a bad sailor I am."

She gave Kelvin Ward an intimate little glance from under her dark eye-lashes, but he appeared not to be looking at her. After a moment he said:

"We were just about to retire to our cabin. Good-night, Auriel. It is pleasant to see you in such good health."

He put his hand as he spoke under Seraphina's arm and led her down the corridor to their State-Room.

When they entered the cabin she busied herself removing the velvet wrap from her shoulders. Kelvin Ward rang for a steward to order coffee for them both and brandy for himself.

"I think I am rather tired," Seraphina said after a moment. "So if you do not mind, when we have drunk our coffee, I will go to bed. There is a concert in the Saloon which you might wish to attend."

"I can imagine nothing which would bore me more," Kelvin Ward replied. "Concerts on board ship are usually hideously dull, or the singers are too bawdy to be anything but an embarrassment."

Seraphina smiled vaguely. She appeared, despite their interesting conversation at dinner, to have little to say.

The steward brought the coffee. While he was still pouring out the brandy and chatting about the weather, she rose to her feet and having said good-night moved into her cabin.

Alone, she made no effort to send for Martha to help her undress.

Instead she sat down at the dressing-table looking at her own reflexion with un-seeing eyes.

She was glad now that the waiter in the Dining-Saloon had prevented her from explaining what had brought the colour to her cheeks.

It was something she had overheard earlier in the day.

For the first time since they left England it had been warm enough in the Mediterranean sunshine to open the port-holes.

Kelvin had left Seraphina alone while he went to play the ship's version of deck tennis, a strenuous game in which rope quoits were used and which proved an excellent way to take exercise.

Seraphina was reading one of her books on India when through the open port-hole she heard voices outside.

The first-class cabins opened on to the promenade deck where the life-boats stood and where usually the more hearty of the passengers took their exercise.

It was however not men's voices Seraphina heard but women's.

She would not have paid any attention had not the first words in dulcet tones been:

"Why did you not tell me that Kelvin Ward was on board?"

"I had no idea you knew him!" another woman's voice replied.

"Not know Kelvin? My dear, you are behind the times! I knew him well—very well indeed, in Bombay last Autumn."

"So it was like that, was it?"

"Very much so, but then unfortunately my father died and I had to go home. These things always seem to happen just at the wrong moment."

"I should have told you he was on board. Indeed the ship has talked of little else, but as he is on his honeymoon I could not think it would particularly interest you, knowing, Auriel, your *penchant* for unattached males!"

The woman called Auriel laughed.

"It would not matter to me if Kelvin had fifty wives. He is without exception the most attractive, alluring, passionate lover I have ever known."

"Auriel! I repeat—he is on his honeymoon."

"Kelvin always swore he would not marry."

"Then he must have changed his mind, for his wife is with him."

"What is she like?"

"Pretty, slightly insignificant, but enormously rich!"

There was a little tinkling laugh which appeared to have another significance besides mirth.

"So much competition!"

"Auriel, you must behave yourself! You know as well as I do that your husband's position in Bombay makes it impossible for you to cause scandal."

"There will be no scandal!"

"I do not like the expression in your eyes."

"Then look elsewhere! I am angry with you— very angry—to think I have wasted so much of the voyage already!"

"There are still nine days of it left."

"Thank goodness! An eternity would not be long enough where Kelvin is concerned!"

"Auriel, you really shock me!"

"I have always done that, Emily. Have you forgotten?"

"No, dear, but Mrs. Ward is a sweet little thing. You may say it is sentimental of me, but I would not like her to be hurt."

"The feelings of Mrs. Ward do not concern me! Only those of her husband! Let us move. It is cold sitting down and I have no intention of being ill again, at any rate not for the next nine days and nights."

Again there was laughter. Then Seraphina heard the ladies who had spoken move away.

She had sat very still thinking over what she had heard.

It seemed very foolish now, but she had never envisaged there might have been other women in her husband's life.

She had been concerned at first only by the fact that he was big and over-powering and she wished to avoid annoying him.

Then she knew that since they had been married she had every day and every hour felt more at ease and in some strange way closer to him.

She had grown to realise that he was a man of deep feelings.

When he scowled as he did when he was angry he still frightened her. But she knew that he meant to be gentle, and his consideration and thought for her was something she had never experienced before.

It was difficult to explain to herself, let alone to him, how strange and at the same time exciting it was for her to be alone with a man, and to know for the first time in her life someone was prepared to ask her opinion; to listen to what she had to say.

She felt herself relaxing, looking forward eagerly when each morning came to being with him.

It was almost as if she were a flower and her petals were unfolding in the sunshine.

Now she saw Kelvin Ward in a different aspect, as a man who attracted other women: a man who, if the anonymous voice was to be believed, was also attracted passionately by them.

Seraphina had never been allowed to read romantic novels, but nevertheless love in some shape or form had crept in, even in the Classics.

There was love in the mythology of ancient Greece and Rome, love in the histories of Kings and Queens, love in the lives of such men as Byron, Reubens and Napoleon.

It should have taught her, she thought now, that men required more than friendship from a woman, and obviously very much more than she was giving her husband.

Her ignorance seemed to her like a fog in

which she could not find her way. Then she tried to think of Kelvin rather than herself.

'Perhaps I am depriving him of what he is entitled to as a man,' she thought.

It was all muddling and incoherent and Seraphina could not make any pattern out of what she thought and felt.

She only knew it was like a maze to which she had no key and in which she was completely and utterly lost.

Then when she met Lady Braithwaite she recognised it was she who had gossiped outside the port-hole of her cabin.

She felt herself sinking into insignificance beside the beauty, the elegance, the poise of the older woman.

She also had not missed the way in which she had held out both her hands and the soft caressing note in her voice.

'If that is the sort of woman Kelvin admires,' Seraphina thought despairingly, 'how will he ever put up with me?'

All the insecurity she had known for so long, all the unsureness of herself which had made her so afraid when her father had told her she was to be married, made her now feel she wanted to run away and hide where nobody could find her.

It was obvious from the conversation which she had over-heard outside her port-hole that Lady Braithwaite was in love with Kelvin and that they had meant something to each other.

'They must have been very intimate,' Seraphina thought, 'before Lady Braithwaite had been forced to return to England.'

He had indeed not appeared to be particularly pleased to see her despite her enthusiastic greeting; but then, Seraphina thought shrewdly, he had been aware that she was aboard while to her it had been a surprise.

He would have had time while the ship was

tossing in the Bay to prepare himself for what must be an unavoidable meeting, and he was therefore not taken off his guard.

'Because I am his wife he will hide from me whatever feelings he has for her,' Seraphina told herself. 'He would not wish me to know what they had meant to each other.

It was the thought of this that had brought the colour to her cheeks when at dinner Kelvin Ward had said:

"If I wanted to hide anything from you it would be difficult."

And yet, Seraphina asked herself, why should they not be honest with each other? Why should he not say to her: "I married you because I was forced to do so, but I am in love with someone else—Lady Braithwaite"?

If he said that what would she do?

Seraphina put her fingers up to her forehead.

'What would be the right thing to do?' she wondered.

Then she told herself this problem must have beset many wives, and obviously the only correct behaviour would be to pretend one noticed nothing.

Without consciously being aware that she did so, Seraphina made a little hopeless gesture with her hands.

In that case their growing frankness with each other, the tie of friendship which had made it easy for her to tell Kelvin anything that came into her mind, would no longer exist.

There would be secrets! Secrets which they dare not speak and which would lie between them like a barrier over which neither of them could climb.

'Why ... why,' Seraphina asked herself, 'just as I am getting to know him, did she have to appear at this moment?'

It was a cry that women had made all down the ages, but Seraphina was not to know it.

She was only aware that something very precious which had been evolving between her and her husband seemed to have slipped away from her, so that she was no longer sure of it.

'Perhaps he will still want to be friends with me,' she told herself and wondered why the thought brought her no elation.

She felt only a sensation not unlike that of despair.

Kelvin Ward, having finished his coffee and brandy, rose to his feet and left the cabin.

He was determined not to run into Auriel Braithwaite if he could help it. Feeling quite certain that she would either be in the Saloon or in the Card-Room, he deliberately climbed to the upper deck of the ship.

It was growing warmer every day and at dawn they would reach Alexandria.

The sky was full of stars and Kelvin Ward walked slowly along the upper deck and back again, feeling a satisfaction in finding he was alone and safe without interruptions.

He stopped at the stern and leaning over the rail looked at the sea.

Then he heard the rustle of silk and was aware who was approaching him before she reached his side.

"Are you hiding from me, Kelvin?" she asked in a voice that had a strange mesmeric note in it which men found irrestible.

"I thought you would be playing cards."

"That was why I was certain I would find you here!" Auriel Braithwaite said with a hint of laughter in her voice.

There was the seductive, exotic fragrance of her perfume which Kelvin Ward remembered all too well.

She was English, but somewhere far back in the years she had had a Russian ancestor and liked to imagine that the mystic characteristics of that unfathomable race had been born again in her.

Auriel Braithwaite managed to infuse an air of secrecy and exoticism into everything she said or did.

At one time it had been a matter of artifice.

Now it had become instinctive, and for the men who loved her—and there had been many of them—there was the strange excitement in having always to interpret from her words or behaviour what she really meant.

"Are you not thrilled to see me again?"

"No!"

"Must you be so ungallant?" she enquired.

"I am a married man, Auriel."

"Should that concern me?"

"It concerns me!"

She laughed very softly.

"Men have been married since Adam! Even so he could not resist Lilith."

"I am on my honeymoon."

She laughed again.

"The perfect, gentle Knight, the Public-School spirit and St. Anthony all rolled into one."

Kelvin Ward straightened himself and looked down at her standing beside him.

She was very alluring and she was well aware of it.

Despite the slight chill of the evening she had let her ermine wrap fall back from her shoulders to reveal the exquisite column of her neck, white and translucent in the light from the stars.

She seemed to glow like the phosphorous on the sea, and her eyes, which slanted up at the corners, glittered an invitation which was echoed in the curve of her lips.

"There is so much more we have to say to each other," she said in a soft voice that was hardly above a whisper. "Unfinished symphonies always leave me restless."

"No, Auriel!"

Kelvin's words were firm and almost hard.

"Have you forgotten what we meant to each other?" Auriel Braithwaite asked. "Have you forgotten that night in the garden when you carried me back to the house where we discovered a thousand delights in each other that I did not even know existed?"

She spoke passionately, moving a little nearer to him as she spoke.

"I said no, Auriel!"

"Why? Why? You say you are married, but what does that signify? You needed money and your wife has provided it. That is understandable. . . ."

Auriel Braithwaite paused for a moment before she said:

"You left India less than a month ago. I am certain you did not know this girl before you reached England. If you did, she meant nothing to you."

Kelvin Ward did not speak and then very, very softly against his ear Auriel Braithwaite murmured:

"Let us finish the symphony, Kelvin."

As she spoke her arms went round his neck.

Before he could move her mouth was on his, her body soft and close against him.

Just for a moment he felt her lips hungry, passionate, demanding. Then gently but firmly he unclasped her arms and put her aside from him.

"I said no, Auriel," he repeated.

Then he turned and walked away down the deck, leaving her staring after him.

He went back into the Sitting-Room and poured himself out another glass of brandy.

He had just raised it to his lips when he heard the door of Seraphina's cabin open. As he turned his head it shut again.

He walked across to the door, knocked and when there was no answer entered.

Seraphina still fully dressed was standing in the centre of the cabin.

He looked at her face and asked:

"What is the matter? Why have you not gone to bed?"

"I . . . thought you had gone . . . out," she said hesitantly. "I . . . did not . . . imagine that you . . . would have come . . . back so . . . quickly."

"What has upset you?" he asked as he had asked before.

She turned her face away from him.

"It . . . it . . . nothing. I . . . I am going . . . to bed."

"Is there any reason why you should not tell me the truth?" he enquired.

"I . . . I was just being . . . foolish."

"About what?"

"I have nothing to . . . tell you," she said. "I just thought you . . . had gone . . . on deck."

"You taught me to be perceptive, Seraphina," Kelvin Ward said. "Now I know that something is disturbing you and I want you to tell me about it."

"I do not . . . think you would . . . understand."

"Will you not try me?"

She still stood indecisively in the centre of the cabin and he sat down on the bed.

"We have discussed a lot of things together," he said quietly, "and you promised to tell me your thoughts and your feelings. Now suddenly you are hiding something from me. Why?"

"It is . . . something . . . I do not . . . understand," Seraphina said. "No. I . . . suppose that is not . . . true. I . . . do understand it but . . ."

Her voice was almost incoherent.

"Let us go back to what we were talking about at dinner," Kelvin Ward said. "You said then there

were things I would not wish you to know. What
sort of things were you thinking about?"

There was silence and after a moment he added:

"I thought we made a pact, Seraphina."

"We ... did," she said unhappily. "I ... I
think this is ... outside it."

"Nothing is outside it, and I mean that."

"Nothing at ... all?"

"Nothing as far as I am concerned."

She looked at him, her eyes very wide and
enquiring in her small face. Then she said:

"If ... if I ask you ... a question ... you will
... not be ... angry?"

"I would never be angry about anything you
asked me."

"Then ... are you ... very much in love ...
with that lady we ... just met?"

Kelvin Ward told himself that this was what
he had half-expected, yet somehow it came as a
shock.

"Who has been talking to you?" he asked.

"No-one," Seraphina replied. "It is just that I
... over-heard a ... conversation ... by mistake."

"When?"

"This afternoon."

"How did you over-hear it and who was
speaking?"

"I opened my port-hole," Seraphina said with
a little gesture of her hand, "but I did not ...
know who it was I heard talking until you ... introduced me to ... Lady Braithwaite."

"I see! And you learnt that she and I had
been acquaintances in the past?"

"She ... she said ... that you were ... attracted by ... each other. It was ... very stupid of me
but I ... had not thought about ... the women
there must have been ... in your ... life."

"And what were you going to say to me at
dinner?"

"I was going to say," Seraphina said, "that because you were ... forced to marry me I ought not to ... stand in your way if you wanted to be with ladies ... who attracted you."

She paused, and glancing at Kelvin Ward a little apprehensively she added:

"That ... was before ... I had seen ... Lady Braithwaite."

"And now that you have seen her?" Kelvin Ward asked quietly.

"She is ... so beautiful, so ... smart and ... sophisticated," Seraphina said. "I ... understand what you must ... feel about her."

There was a pathetically lost note in her voice which Kelvin Ward did not miss.

"Come and sit down beside me, Seraphina," he said. "I want to explain something to you."

She looked at him nervously but she obeyed him.

He did not touch her and she sat beside him on the bed.

After a moment he said:

"I am a good deal older than you, Seraphina. I have been a bachelor for many years and I would not insult your intelligence by pretending that I had not had a number of what people call 'love affairs' in my life."

"Yes ... of course," she murmured.

"They are a game a man plays with attractive women who realise that it is not serious enough to entail their running away from their husbands or doing anything which would cause a scandal, and which is for them both extremely amusing."

Seraphina's eyes were on his face and she was listening intently.

"And while these love affairs are sometimes just flirtations," Kelvin Ward went on, "or perhaps more passionate interludes, at the same time a man keeps a very special place in his heart for the woman who will one day become his wife and the mother of his children."

"You mean there is a difference?" Seraphina said.

"A very important difference," Kelvin Ward replied. "Let me explain this to you, Seraphina. A man, if he is a gentleman, does not indulge in love affairs with young, unsophisticated girls or women who do not know what they are doing."

He paused to say firmly:

"In fact it is as I have already said, a game in which according to the unwritten rules no-one should be hurt."

"And yet people are hurt?" Seraphina said questioningly.

"Sometimes. And that is regrettable," Kelvin Ward replied. "But in most cases after what the French call an *'affaire de coeur'* the man and woman in question part without rancour, or become friends."

He paused and said slowly:

"When they look back on what happened they remember it only as a charming and attractive interlude in their lives which made them for a short time very happy, but which they were both aware could have no permanence."

"I . . . I think . . . I . . . understand," Seraphina said. "And that . . . is what you felt for Lady Braithwaite?"

"Exactly!" Kelvin Ward answered.

"When she . . . spoke of you and I . . . overheard what she . . . said," Seraphina said hesitatingly, "she . . . did not . . . t-talk as if you were someone in the . . . past."

Kelvin Ward's lips tightened for a moment.

Why of all places which Auriel Braithwaite might have chosen to discuss him, had it to be outside Seraphina's port-hole?

He answered quietly:

"Without being at all unkind, Seraphina, I

think you will understand when I say that Auriel Braithwaite is the type of woman who likes to feel that she is the one to finish first when the game is over."

There was silence and then at last Seraphina said in a small voice:

"Thank you ... for explaining these ... things ... to me. I will try not to ... make mistakes, but she makes me feel ... as if I am ... nothing ... a ... nobody."

"You are my wife, Seraphina," Kelvin Ward said firmly, "and let me say this in all honesty: I have never met anyone in the whole of my life before who knows so much about the things which really matter."

She lifted her eyes to his and he went on very gently:

"We both of us know there are many different types of knowledge, just as there are many different types of love. I think in the last few days you and I have found our minds journeying together down strange roads and up the sides of unexplored mountains. Does that mean nothing to you?"

"It means everything. So much ... more than I can ... ever explain," Seraphina said quickly.

"Then think about that and not the other things that puzzle you," Kelvin Ward said. "And now I suggest you go to bed, as I am going to do."

"You are ... not going out on deck again?"

"No. I am going to bed. If you leave your door open you will see my lights go out."

"You know if you tell me something ... I believe you," Seraphina said with an unexpected dignity.

"Of course," he smiled. "There is honesty between friends and we are still friends, Seraphina?"

It was a question.

"Yes, of course," she answered. "And just as a friend would do, you have smoothed out the puzzle and I am no longer in a maze."

"I told you that you should trust me," he answered.

Then he went from the cabin, closing the door behind him.

The following evening they left Alexandria, and when they reached Port Said a day later Seraphina was to find that her husband was at her side showing her the different sights and explaining to her much that she wanted to know.

Never, she thought, had she imagined there could be so many ships as there were waiting to pass through the famous Canal which opened in 1869 and was now the vulnerable artery connecting East and West.

Although half the Australian traffic still used the Cape route and other ships went round the Horn, all ships on the homeward passage when loaded with perishable cargo used the Canal.

"The British Government owns shares in the Canal Company from the Khedive of Egypt," Kelvin Ward told Seraphina, "and the defence of it is the responsibility of the British Garrison in Egypt."

"But I believe they all pay something similar to a toll-charge," Seraphina said.

"That is true," Kelvin Ward answered with a smile. "The Royal Mail steam-ships actually have priority of traffic, and the big Indian liners regularly pay up to one thousand pounds in dues."

"Who gets the money?" Seraphina asked.

"The profits are divided between the shareholders," Kelvin Ward replied. "There is unfortunately sixty-five million pounds of French capital compared with only thirty-one million British so there are twenty-one French Directors to ten British and one Dutch."

He laughed.

"Needless to say they constantly squabble

about transit fees. The British always want them lower—the French higher!"

He went on to explain that the Canal was too small for British Imperial requirements.

"Large battle-ships," he said, "can only go through by dismantling their heavy guns."

"Why have they not enlarged it?" Seraphina asked.

"It sounds a practical solution," he replied, "and sometimes the British have thought of cutting a rival Canal through the Sinai Peninsula, but I have the uncomfortable feeling that nothing will be done!"

When they were moving about the deck and talking at meal-times, Seraphina was aware that Lady Braithwaite was watching them, and there was an unpleasant expression in her flashing dark eyes.

She was certain that here was an enemy who could be dangerous if she had the chance, and she wondered if Kelvin was aware of the enmity they had aroused.

'She loves him,' Seraphina told herself.

The idea was very depressing.

Because she could never control her imagination, she found herself lying awake at night wondering what would happen if someday Kelvin came to her and told her frankly he wanted to be free.

Supposing he found the woman he had always visualised he might love?

It would not be a question then of a flirtation that was only a game, but of losing him completely.

She was aware of how angry it would make her father, and she could almost see herself fighting to protect Kelvin from Sir Erasmus's wrath.

Then she told herself she was torturing herself unnecessarily.

Kelvin seemed content with her. He was kind. Kinder these past days than he had been before. Or

perhaps it was because she so desperately needed
the reassurance of his company and was metaphori-
cally if not actually holding on to him for fear
Lady Braithwaite would take him from her.

'I will not let her have him!' Seraphina told
herself and then wondered despairingly what weapons she could utilise in a fight.

Without meaning to do so she watched Lady
Braithwaite when they were within sight of each
other.

She could not help admiring the manner in
which she entered the Dining-Saloon.

Almost like a prima donna taking the centre
of the stage she swept to her seat glittering with
jewels and wearing gowns calculated to arouse the
envy of every woman who saw them.

Seraphina had discovered that Lady Braithwaite's husband was the General commanding
Bombay.

It had not been difficult to learn from the
other ladies with whom she sometimes passed the
time of day that General Sir Reginald Braithwaite
was very much older than his wife and was considered a dull, somewhat prosaic man who had few if
any interests outside his Army life.

"Lady Braithwaite is noted as being very
gay!" one elderly passenger said acidly, with
pursed lips.

Seraphina with a little sigh knew exactly what
was meant by that.

Amongst the first-class passengers there were
few Indians, but there were a party of them in a
suite not far from their own who interested Seraphina because they so seldom appeared.

When she enquired who the ladies were she
learnt that it was Her Highness the Rajmata of
Udaipur who was returning to India from England.

"What does Rajmata mean?" she asked her
husband.

"It means the mother of a Maharajah," he answered, "or in this case, the Maharana."

"I would so much like to meet her," Seraphina said eagerly.

"I think it is unlikely you will have the opportunity," Kelvin Ward replied and she had to be content with that.

However, when they reached the Red Sea and it was very hot, Seraphina spent much more time on deck than she had done before.

The first-class deck was above the second-class. Below again was the third or steerage, where the passengers sat, played or slept at night at the stern of the ship.

It did not look very comfortable as they had to insert themselves between piles of ropes and the super-structure so there was very little room. Despite this they appeared to enjoy themselves.

Seraphina leaning over the rail would hear music from an Indian sitar or watch Indian children with their brown skins and liquid dark eyes running about amongst the recumbent figures of men and women who appeared quite unconcerned by the noise.

"Why do they interest you so much?" Kelvin asked after Seraphina had watched for a long time what was happening below.

"I think because they are Indians," she answered. "I have been reading my books and I am looking forward more than I can say to seeing what appears to be a very beautiful country and getting to know its people."

"I want you to like India," he said. "If it pleased you we would settle there for some years."

He saw the sudden flash in her eyes and said quickly:

"Do not say anything now. I do not want you to commit yourself, but when you have been in India for some months, you shall tell me what you feel about it."

"I know already that I shall love it as you do," Seraphina answered.

It was very hot that evening. After dinner they walked along the top deck and Seraphina did not even need a wrap over her evening gown.

Tonight she wore soft pink crêpe trimmed with frills of tulle which cascaded behind her from a large satin bow to make a small bustle which ended in a train.

She looked like a rose-bud and it was, Kelvin Ward knew, the very latest fashion from Paris.

It was becoming to Seraphina particularly because in front the gown was tightly moulded to her slight but exquisitely curved figure. While the white perfection of her neck was revealed by the off-the-shoulder décolletage.

Martha had arranged several diamond stars in Seraphina's fair hair, and she seemed to Kelvin Ward to be almost part of the star-strewn Heavens and the moon which threw a silver light over the smooth sea.

There was only the chuff-chuff of the engines and far away in the distance the sound of violins coming from the first-class Saloon.

Below them in the stern there was no music. Instead Seraphina saw a number of soldiers had joined the Indians and their children.

The soldiers were being noisy and rough. They had a football and were throwing it from one to the other, jostling to get it and even knocking one another over.

"I have an idea that the beer is flowing rather too freely," Kelvin Ward said dryly.

"You mean they are drunk?" Seraphina asked.

"Not drunk. Not as a soldier knows the word! But they will be aggressive and perhaps riotous and the Indians, who do not drink, find it difficult to understand the white man when he has imbibed rather too freely!"

Seraphina peered down below.

The soldiers were certainly loud-mouthed and uncouth.

One of them threw the football high in the air and another to prevent it going over-board leapt to save it, then fell heavily against a small Indian child who had been watching them.

The child fell to the deck with a shrill cry.

"That soldier has hurt the child," Seraphina said as the man was pulled to his feet by his companions.

They turned away laughing and joking amongst themselves to disappear.

The Indian child lay where it had fallen in the shadows and Seraphina saw that it did not move.

"The child has been knocked unconscious," she said.

"I am sure someone will realise it is hurt," Kelvin Ward replied.

"Nobody appears to have seen what happened."

It was true that the steerage passengers were sitting on the other side of the ship, which was out of the wind.

The child still lay where it had fallen.

"We must go and tell someone it is hurt—for I am sure it is," Seraphina said.

"I will go," Kelvin answered.

"Please let me come with you."

"There is no reason for you to do so," he replied. "I will do everything that is necessary."

"I want to come. I shall worry about the child if I do not see that it is properly attended to. So please, please take me with you."

Kelvin Ward had appeared almost adamant against her accompanying him. Now unexpectedly he smiled.

"Come along then," he said. "We will go together, but I expect we shall find when we get there you have been over-anxious."

Seraphina slipped her hand in his.

"Let us go quickly," she said.

Good-humouredly holding his wife's hand, Kelvin Ward led her the quickest way down the stairs from the first-class deck to the steerage.

It took a little time but finally with Seraphina lifting the full folds of her tulle train in her hands they stepped onto the open deck in the stern.

There was no sign of the soldiers, and the passengers on the other side were still asleep and quite oblivious of the child still lying where it had fallen.

Seraphina ran forward and knelt down.

She saw a little Indian girl, her dark hair parted down the centre and drawn back with red ribbons. She wore small gold ear-rings but her dress was skimpy and of poor material.

"She must have hit her head when she fell and is unconscious," Seraphina said.

"We must find out where her parents are," Kelvin Ward replied.

Seraphina lifted the child into her arms, then gave an exclamation.

"Look at her arm! Oh, Kelvin, she must have broken it when she fell!"

The little girl's arm certainly seemed to lie at a very strange angle.

"Do not move her," he said sharply. "I will find a steward and then we will get the Doctor."

Seraphina with her pink gown billowing out on the deck around her held the child a little closer.

She was very small and thin and Seraphina guessed that she would be five or six years of age.

A sailor came across the deck and looked at them in astonishment but did not speak and disappeared again.

It was some time before Kelvin Ward returned with a steward.

He was followed by an Indian woman, her sari pulled over her head, a caste mark on her forehead.

She knelt down beside Seraphina and seeing the child's eyes were closed started to wail.

"She is all right!" Seraphina said hastily. "She is not dead—only unconscious."

The woman obviously did not understand.

"Please explain to her, Kelvin."

He spoke some words in Hindi and the woman stopped crying.

"I have found their cabin," he said. "It is rather over-crowded but we had better carry the child there; then we will fetch the Doctor."

"Pick her up very gently," Seraphina warned. "I am certain the arm is broken."

Kelvin Ward took the child from Seraphina's arms.

The door into the ship was opened for him and moving slowly so as not to hurt the still-unconscious little girl, he carried her along the labyrinth of corridors until finally they stopped outside a cabin.

The steward opened the door and Seraphina looked inside with horror.

There were six children, a very old woman and a man all in a cabin which had only four berths.

Some of the children, it was true, seemed tiny, but she saw there was no chance of the injured girl having a bed to herself.

Kelvin Ward asked the steward if there was an empty cabin.

"I will pay for one," he said.

"There's one vacant on the other side of the corridor, Sir," the steward answered. "It was occupied until we reached Alexandria."

"Then open the door," Kelvin Ward ordered.

The cabin was very small and had no outside port-hole but at least there was room for the child to have a bunk to herself.

Very gently Kelvin Ward laid her down on it. Her eyes opened and she began to whimper.

Her mother moved to her side.

"Tell her on no account to move the little

girl's arm until we can find the Doctor," Seraphina said.

As she spoke she took a pillow from one of the other bunks and propped the child's injured elbow upon it.

"We will bring the Doctor back immediately," Kelvin Ward said to the steward, "and tell the Purser to let me have the bill for this cabin."

"Very good, Sir."

Kelvin Ward said something in Hindi to the mother.

By this time they had been joined by an Indian man who was obviously the father of the child, and the old woman in the other cabin whom Seraphina suspected of being the grandmother.

Hastily they climbed the stairs back to the first-class deck.

"I know where the Doctor's Surgery is," Kelvin Ward said.

He led the way to it and knocked on the door.

Seraphina remembered that the Doctor was a red-faced, jovial man who had introduced himself to her during the storm in the Bay of Biscay.

"I am glad to see you on your feet, Mrs. Ward," he had said. "But do be careful not to get thrown about by the heavy sea. I have no wish to add to my complement of patients."

"I am afraid you are very busy, Doctor," Kelvin Ward had said.

"Far too busy for my liking!" the Doctor replied.

Seraphina guessed him to be a lazy man for he certainly took his duties lightly. Whenever they passed the Smoking-Room where there was a Bar, he was always there.

He had a loud laugh which was unmistakable.

Kelvin Ward knocked at the door of the Surgery. There was no answer and he knocked again.

"I expect he is at the Bar," he said. "I shall have to go and look for him there."

They turned and walked back along the corridor.

As they did so they saw three people approaching them from the other end.

As they advanced Seraphina realised that the three people consisted of the Doctor in the centre, who, with his arms round the shoulders of two stewards, was being supported by them.

His face was very red, his eyes were closed and his head slumped forward on his chest.

He was murmuring something to himself which did not seem to make sense, and as they reached him Seraphina realised that his feet hardly touched the ground. The stewards were carrying him.

Seraphina and Kelvin Ward flattened themselves against the side of the corridor so that the Doctor and his attendants could pass.

"I hardly think that the Doctor is in a fit state to set a child's arm!" Kelvin Ward said dryly.

"Then what can we do?" Seraphina asked, her eyes very wide.

"I am afraid she will have to wait until the morning," he replied.

"Until morning?" Seraphina repeated. "But that is impossible! When she regains consciousness she will be in an agony of pain. I broke my own arm once and I know what it feels like!"

"I will ask the Purser," Kelvin Ward said. "But I doubt if there will be anyone else qualified to deal with it. If it is badly set the child might have a stiff arm for the rest of her life!"

Seraphina stood still, her eyes troubled.

"Something has to be done!" she said positively. "The child cannot suffer in such a way. Besides, by the morning the arm will be very swollen."

By this time they had reached the centre of the first-class deck.

On their right was the Saloon.

Unexpectedly, without saying anything, Seraphina left Kelvin Ward's side and walked into the big room.

Its red velvet chairs were filled with passengers and the Orchestra was playing softly.

To Kelvin Ward's astonishment Seraphina went up to the small platform on which the Orchestra was playing and held up her hand.

"Will you please stop for a moment?" she asked.

The cessation of the music and the sound of her voice brought a sudden silence to the assembled company.

Every head turned in her direction.

Seraphina drew in her breath then said in a clear, audible tone:

"There has been an accident to a child. I think her arm is broken but the Doctor is ill. Is there anyone here qualified to attend to her?"

There was a moment's silence, then from the far end of the room an elderly man in evening dress rose to his feet.

"I am a Doctor," he said. "I am retired but still capable of carrying out my duties."

"Thank you," Seraphina said simply. "Will you please come at once?"

Chapter Five

Kelvin Ward returning to his cabin after a strenuous game of deck tennis found Seraphina waiting for him with a look of excitement in her eyes.

"Oh, Kelvin, what do you think has happened?" she asked as he entered.

"It is obviously something pleasant!" he said with a smile.

He saw that her whole face was illuminated and her eyes were sparkling.

"It is!" she replied. "A dear old man, an Indian, knocked on the door a few moments ago and asked if I would honour Her Highness the Rajmata of Udaipur by having tea with her."

"That is what you wanted, was it not?" Kelvin Ward said.

"I cannot think why she has asked me," Seraphina went on, "but I accepted. You do not mind my having done so?"

"No, of course not," he answered. "It will be very interesting for you and I am delighted that your first invitation to the Indian people should be by meeting one of India's oldest Dynasties."

"Tell me about them," Seraphina begged.

"The Maharana of Udaipur is Chief of 'Thirty-six Royal Tribes.' The house of Mewar is the only Dynasty in India which still rules over the same territory as its ancestors ruled for centuries before the Muhammadan invaders first crossed the Indus."

"They are Rajputs, are they not?" Seraphina asked with a glance at the books she had been studying since she came aboard.

"The Rajputs are the most romantic and interesting of the Indian tribes," Kelvin Ward answered. "They believe that they descend from the sun, the moon and divine fire."

"How exciting!"

"In chivalry and courage they seem to have equalled the Mediaeval Knights," Kelvin Ward continued, "and they enjoyed war!"

He smiled.

"If there were no wars, they hunted, but they preferred a war and if no other enemy could be found, they would fight each other!"

"My book says that they were a very handsome people," Seraphina said.

"Their Princesses were renowned for their beauty and also for their daring and their independence," Kelvin Ward went on. "Unlike the rest of the women in India, they married where they chose and went hunting with their men. They even followed them into battle!"

"They must have been very brave!"

"They were braver still when they proudly threw themselves on their husband's funeral pyres and committed *sutee*. But that has now been forbidden by the British."

Seraphina shuddered.

"Despite their emancipated behaviour," Kelvin Ward continued, "the Princes knew how to manage their women. In their Palaces there was a room called the 'Anger Chamber' where a Princess could be shut away until she apologised for her rage!"

Seraphina laughed.

"What happened if the Prince or Maharajah was angry?"

"He was and is a Maharana, which is grander. But of course he was allowed to behave as he pleased, as all men must be allowed to do!" Kelvin Ward teased.

"You are very arrogant and autocratic," Seraphina retorted. "Have women no rights?"

"Only those of trying to please their Lords and Masters!"

"You are not a Rajput!"

"I wish I were! They are very remarkable men."

"In what way?" Seraphina asked.

"They would never admit defeat. It was the Rajputs alone among the Hindu Princes of Northern India who kept up the struggle against the Moslems, and if ever a battle went against them their wives and mothers would not receive them on their return home."

"Which makes me more eager than ever to meet the Rajmata," Seraphina said.

"She will have been a Rajput Princess, and therefore in her youth very beautiful," Kelvin Ward told her.

"Do not make me nervous," Seraphina begged, "or I shall be afraid to go to tea with her."

"You nervous?" Kelvin Ward asked. "I shall never believe that after the way you behaved the night before last."

Seraphina blushed.

Kelvin Ward had teased her ever since she had asked for a Doctor to set the arm of the Indian child.

When they had taken the retired Doctor from

the Saloon down to the child's cabin, Kelvin Ward
had insisted on Seraphina leaving him to set the
arm without her being present.

"It will upset you," he said gently. "Dr.
Brownlow tells me that he has practised in Harley
Street and I am quite sure you can leave every-
thing in his hands without worrying."

Obediently Seraphina had gone back to their
own cabin and later a message had come to say
that the child was quite comfortable and that the
Doctor had given her something to make her sleep.

But when she was alone again with her husband it seemed as if Seraphina realised for the first
time that she had behaved in what was an unexpected manner and she looked at Kelvin nervously.

"Y-you are . . . not angry . . . with me for
trying to . . . find someone who could help the . . .
child?" she asked in a low voice.

"Of course I am not!" he replied. "At the
same time I am wondering what happened to the
young woman who was afraid of a storm at sea and
who told me she was a coward!"

"I forgot about . . . myself," Seraphina explained simply. "I was so . . . worried about the . . .
child suffering so much pain that . . . I simply had
to . . . do something."

"And very effectively!" Kelvin Ward com-
mended. "I still think it was very brave of you to
stand up in the Saloon, stop the band and ask for a
Doctor."

The following day they had gone down to the
steerage to find out if there was anything they
could do for the little Indian girl.

There were no toys to be bought on board, but
Seraphina found some coloured wool, three red,
pink and blue handkerchiefs and other small objects amongst her luggage with which a child could
play.

She had not been mistaken. The little Indian
girl was delighted with them, and both the father

and mother thanked her profusely for her kindness. The father spoke excellent English.

"They seem to be very poor," Seraphina said to Kelvin Ward later. "How can they manage to travel in a fine ship like this even in the third class?"

"The man was working for an Indian company in England and was allowed to have his wife with him," Kelvin Ward replied. "Their children have all been born in England, and now after ten years they have saved enough to return to their own country."

"What will they do when they get there?" Seraphina enquired.

"I imagine he will try to get another job, and until he does they will live in very crowded conditions with their relations."

"I cannot imagine that they will be particularly welcome arriving with seven children!" Seraphina said.

"The Indian people have a great sense of family," Kelvin Ward answered. "I assure you they will be looked after and welcomed in the family circle from the moment they set foot on their own soil."

When they got back to their own cabin Kelvin said:

"We must find a present for you to take to Her Highness."

"A present?" Seraphina questioned.

"In the East a guest always offers his host or hostess a gift."

"What a delightful idea!" Seraphina exclaimed. "What can I give the Rajmata?"

After much discussion they decided on a pretty little antique box which had been a wedding present. Seraphina wrapped it in tissue paper and tied it with a piece of red ribbon.

Kelvin Ward had the idea that Seraphina had

been asked to tea with the Rajmata because of her kindness to the Indian child. He was not mistaken.

The Rajmata, Seraphina found on entering the cabin, was unable to rise from a wheel-chair in which she was sitting.

When she had made the Indian greeting of a *Namashar*, which means both hands joined together fingers to fingers and palm to palm, the Rajmata said in perfect English:

"You must excuse me, Mrs. Ward, for being unable to rise to greet you, but I am unfortunately incapacitated with arthritis in my legs."

She must have been exceedingly beautiful when young, Seraphina thought.

She had the strong clear-cut features and high-bridged nose which Seraphina had seen in Indian paintings and which gave her face an expression of great pride.

Her hair, which must have once been long and thick, was now white, and she wore an exquisitely embroidered sari of deep pink which glittered and shone with every movement she made.

Her bracelets and rings as well as the necklace round her neck were set with rubies and diamonds. Seraphina thought that even if she had not known the Rajmata was Royal, she would have guessed it at first glance.

Her Highness was attended by another woman almost as elderly as herself and an aged man whom Seraphina learnt during the visit was a Courtier of great distinction who had been detailed to escort Her Highness to England.

"We made this long journey," the Rajmata explained, "because my little grandson had to have an eye operation. We were told there was no-one who could do it as well as a British Surgeon, and I am glad to say that the journey has in fact been more than justified."

"Oh, I am so pleased!" Seraphina said. "May I see the little Prince?"

The child, who was nearly two years old, was carried into the cabin.

Seraphina noticed that his *Ayah* was a comparatively young woman and very much in awe of the Rajmata.

The child still had one eye bandaged but he looked in fairly good health and sitting on his grandmother's lap played happily with her bracelets.

"What is the Prince's name?" Seraphina asked.

"His Highness is called Akbar after his illustrious ancestor," the Rajmata replied.

"Is he the Maharana's eldest son?" Seraphina enquired.

"His Highness is the heir—the Maharaj Kumar," the Rajmata answered. "One day he will be called 'The Sun of the Hindus.' "

There was a deep pride in the Princess's voice.

"I have read a little of your history," Seraphina said, "and my husband has told me how brave the Rajputs are."

"Their feuds and wars made a wilderness of our country until we came under the protection of the British in 1817," the Rajmata replied. "Now we have peace."

"I am glad," Seraphina said.

"Will this be your first visit to India, Mrs. Ward?" the Rajmata asked.

"Yes. I am so looking forward to seeing India," Seraphina answered. "My husband loves it deeply, and I have been trying to learn about its people."

"It is because of your kindness to one of our people, Mrs. Ward," the Rajmata said, "that I asked if you would honour me with your presence here this afternoon."

Seraphina smiled.

"You mean the little Indian girl who broke her arm?"

"I was told how much you did for her," the Rajmata said, "and that your husband has provided her with a special cabin. It is indeed very gracious."

"I think really we should be apologising because it was a British soldier who knocked her down," Seraphina said. "But I do not think he realised what he had done."

"That is what I was told," the Rajmata said.

Seraphina had the idea that every detail of the episode had been repeated and repeated so that the old lady knew everything.

They talked of where Udaipur was situated and the Rajmata said as Seraphina left:

"I hope that your husband will find the time to bring you to Rajasthan. It is very beautiful in the Spring and considered to be one of the most picturesque regions of India."

"I have been told," Seraphina answered, "that it is a place of legend and romance, and of Princes who were like the European Knights of Chivalry!"

"I hope when you see it you will not be disappointed," the Rajmata said with a smile.

They had been served while they talked with special little cakes and sweet-meats which were unlike anything Seraphina had tasted before.

Then when the Rajmata sent the Prince with his *Ayah* away to their cabin, Seraphina felt it was time for her to leave.

"Thank you very much for inviting me, Your Highness," she said. "I had so much hoped to meet you."

"I am sure that we will meet again," the Rajmata said. "In gratitude for all you have done we touch your feet."

As everyone raised their hands in a *Namashar*, Seraphina curtseyed and left the cabin.

"Her Highness is beautiful!" she told Kelvin Ward when he asked her how she had got on. "As beautiful as you told me she would be. I hope when I am old I shall look like that!"

"That is a long time away," he answered.

Seraphina wished that he had said that he was certain she would be beautiful, until she realised with a little pang of her heart that he would not say anything that was not true.

How was there any possibility of his thinking her beautiful when he compared her with Lady Braithwaite?

Despite all he had said to reassure her, Seraphina could not help wondering as they journeyed through the Indian Ocean whether Kelvin Ward was in fact meeting Lady Braithwaite without her being aware of it.

It would be so easy when he left her to play deck-tennis or to walk round and round the deck because he felt he must take some exercise for Lady Braithwaite and him to talk together.

Perhaps Lady Braithwaite was using her exotic fascination to bring him close to her again as he had been before.

Yet Kelvin had told her their love affair was over.

Seraphina saw nonetheless the dark smouldering glances Lady Braithwaite gave Kelvin when they were in the Dining-Saloon or passed each other in the corridor.

She was sure that as far as Her Ladyship was concerned, she still desired the man whom she had described as an 'attractive, alluring, passionate lover.'

Kelvin would have kissed her, Seraphina realised, and she wondered what it would be like to feel his lips on hers.

She had always thought in her imagination that kisses were soft and gentle. Now she was not sure.

There was something very strong and masculine about Kelvin, and she had the feeling that his lips might be strong and demanding, although what they demanded she had no idea.

What was meant by a 'passionate lover'?

She went to the ship's Library to try to find a book that would tell her something about love.

There was nothing there which seemed to her to be in the least helpful.

The novels were all rather stilted tales. The men and their women behaved, it seemed to Seraphina, in a manner which bore no relation to real life, and the rest of the Library seemed to consist of books on travel or biographies of Statesmen and Generals long since dead.

She had an almost crazy impulse that evening when they were walking round the deck after dinner to ask Kelvin to kiss her so that she would know what it was like.

Would he understand that she was just being curious?

Then she told herself he would think it an extraordinary request, and she was quite certain that no woman with any sense of propriety would ask a gentleman to kiss her.

'Friends do not kiss . . . not like that!' she said to herself.

But she thought that it would be exciting if Kelvin approached her not as a friend but as a lover.

Then she blushed at the unseemliness of such a thought.

'And yet,' she asked herself, 'he is my husband, so how could it be wrong?'

Nevertheless, Kelvin, so proud, upright and good, had been Lady Braithwaite's lover.

"I do not understand," Seraphina said miserably.

Then she told herself she was being very self-centred and greedy in wanting more when she had so much already.

Her father might easily have married her to a

man who showed her no consideration whatsoever. A man who might have laughed at her for being afraid; a man who would not be in the slightest interested in what she thought and who considered her opinions, as her father did, as something to be ignored.

"I have been lucky ... very lucky," Seraphina whispered.

Yet despite every resolution she somehow felt a feeling of dissatisfaction; something within herself asked for more.

It was hot by the time they were nearing the end of their voyage.

The ladies carried their fans with them and when walking on the deck shaded themselves from the sun with small, elegant sun-shades brought into fashion by Queen Victoria.

Seraphina's dresses in gay colours and made of Indian muslin made Kelvin Ward congratulate her on her appearance and she looked up at him with shining eyes.

"Do you really think I look nice? You are not just saying it out of politeness?"

"I thought we agreed we would tell each other the truth," he answered. "Let me say it again so that you will be quite certain I mean it, Seraphina. You look very pretty—or perhaps the right word is lovely."

Their eyes met and Seraphina felt something very strange and magnetic pass between them.

It was almost as if he drew her towards him, and then before she could describe it to herself or know what she felt, he turned away.

"We shall reach Bombay Harbour this afternoon," he said. "Have you got everything packed?"

"Martha has been packing for two days!" Seraphina answered, "and grumbling all the time she does it!"

Kelvin Ward laughed.

"I have a feeling," he said, "that Martha will demand to go home almost as soon as we arrive."

"She is already threatening to leave."

"I will get you an Indian maid," Kelvin Ward told her. "English servants are a great mistake in an Indian household. They are either insufferably autocratic and expect more waiting on than the Master or Mistress, or else they insist on doing everything themselves, which upsets the whole hierarchy of the caste system."

"You will have to explain that to me sometime," Seraphina said. "I do not want to make mistakes."

"I will prevent you from doing that," he answered.

She felt there was something protective in his voice which made her feel warm and happy inside.

Later, as the heat of the day was cooling a little, Seraphina, standing on deck, saw in the distance the faint outline of land.

"The storm in the Bay has made us later than the Captain anticipated," Kelvin Ward said beside her. "I am afraid it will be dark before we get ashore and I did so want your first impression of India to be of the colourful scene in the streets, which makes it quite different from any other place in the world."

"You must show it to me tomorrow," Seraphina said, then wondered if he would have time for her.

She was well aware that he was itching to reach Bombay to see about his ships and hear the latest news of his company.

He was to become a Senior Partner because he had been able to invest more money than he had originally envisaged.

She glanced at him sideways as he stared out towards the faint blue outline of the land just showing on the horizon.

'He is very handsome!' Seraphina told herself.

She felt that there was something noble in the squareness of his forehead. His grey eyes were penetrating in a way she had never noticed in any man she had met before.

There was so much frankness in them, or perhaps the word she wanted was honesty, that one could not imagine Kelvin Ward doing anything deceitful or underhand, or indeed making a sharp or somewhat shady deal in the interests of business.

'Perhaps he will never make a very good businessman,' Seraphina thought and was glad because it somehow set him apart from the tycoons whom she had met with her father.

"I suppose I had better go and find out what time we shall actually dock," Kelvin Ward said.

"Yes, do that," Seraphina replied. "I will go and see if Martha has finished, but I will not tell her that land is in sight or she will be in a panic!"

"I will join you in a few moments," Kelvin Ward said.

Seraphina went back to the cabin.

Now that all their personal belongings had been packed it somehow looked bare.

So much had happened during the voyage, she thought. It was strange to think that the walls which had enclosed them for twenty days would now pass out of their lives and in the future they would never even remember them.

'We do not even leave an imprint of ourselves,' Seraphina thought. 'It is different in the case of a house.'

Yet, she thought, there were people who lived in a house for years, but because they were non-descript and lacking in personality or character, when they had moved the house became anonymous.

The atmosphere did not change or become enriched through their residing there. There remained only the bricks and mortar.

'A house should be so much more,' she thought, 'especially if it is a home.'

She resolved that when she and Kelvin Ward had a house of their own she would try with every means in her power to make it a place of happiness and comfort. It would be somewhere where he would not only feel he belonged, but which was in every sense of the word a home.

She had, however, the uncomfortable feeling that when they reached Bombay her father would in some manner over-shadow them again and Kelvin would be annoyed.

Perhaps the ships her father had sent would be there before him and that in itself would make him angry.

She felt herself tremble a little at the thought of his anger. Then she told herself they now had an understanding between them, so perhaps he would not be angry with her over something she could not prevent.

Then she remembered that it was her money Kelvin was spending.

It was her money which he must draw on, not only for his company but for their living expenses every day and for everything they did.

'If only he could have some of his own,' she thought.

With a perception she could not evade she knew that every time Kelvin wrote a cheque on her account, he would resent it, and every time he bought something for her he would remember that she had in fact paid for it.

'I hate money! I hate it!' Seraphina told herself.

Then the thought came to her that without it her husband would not have married her.

"I must try to make him forget that I am rich," she whispered.

Then insidiously creeping into her mind came the thought that what Lady Braithwaite had given him could not be translated into terms of money, and he had been able to accept it willingly, eagerly, without rancour.

Kelvin Ward came back into the room.

"They say it will be over an hour before we are able to land," he said. "I have ordered myself a drink. I thought you might like some lemonade."

"Thank you," Seraphina said, forcing a smile to her lips.

"It is no use hanging about on deck," Kelvin said. "That is what people always do and it merely makes one tired and weary long before one has the chance of stepping ashore."

"We will stay here," Seraphina said.

"Everything has been arranged for our arrival and we will be met," Kelvin Ward told her. "I also cabled one of my partners in the company to find us a house. Hotels are usually crowded and uncomfortable, and I thought we could rent a house for a few months to give us time to look around and find something we really like."

"That will be wonderful!" Seraphina cried. "I would much rather have a house of our own than stay at a Hotel."

"Then I am quite sure we will find one waiting for us," Kelvin Ward said. "Do you think you will make a good housekeeper?"

"I hope so," Seraphina replied.

"Do not look so worried," he smiled. "Everything in India is catered for. We shall have a house-boy who will supervise everything. He will engage the other servants, most of whom will turn out to be his relatives. All you will have to do is to give orders and look pretty!"

"I want to make you comfortable," Seraphina said.

"I am sure you will do that," he replied reassuringly.

The steward brought the drink and Kelvin Ward picked up some papers he was studying and which Seraphina was certain related to his company.

She did not interrupt him by chattering idly, but she watched him from under her eyelashes and thought again how attractive he was.

'There must be many, many women who think the same thing!' she thought with a sigh.

Suddenly there was the sound of feet running down the corridor and bells ringing and voices shouting.

Kelvin Ward raised his head.

"What could have happened?" he asked.

"Something seems to be wrong," Seraphina replied.

He rose to open the door.

The noise outside was almost deafening.

He disappeared, leaving Seraphina alone in the cabin.

'What could have happened?' she wondered.

She went into her bed-room expecting to find Martha there but there were only the trunks neatly corded.

Seraphina had already changed from the cool muslin dress into one of heavy silk which Martha thought appropriate for travelling.

Waiting for her on the bed were a heavy silk shawl in which she was to go ashore and her bonnet.

She looked at them, hoping as she felt hot that she would not have to put them on until the last moment, when she heard the Sitting-Room door open and Kelvin's voice.

"Where are you, Seraphina?"

"I am here," she answered.

He came into the bed-room, picked up the shawl from the bed and put it round her shoulders.

"There is no need to be frightened," he said in a quiet grave voice, "but we may have to take to the boats!"

"To the . . . boats?" Seraphina exclaimed in astonishment.

"A fire has broken out on board," he said. "It may be nothing serious. We may be able to remain on the ship, but whatever happens there is no need for you to be afraid. Bombay is within sight and there are dozens of ships to come to our rescue."

"Y-yes," Seraphina said with a little tremor in her voice.

With his arm round her shoulders Kelvin Ward opened the door to take her outside into the corridor.

It seemed to be packed with people jostling, shouting and pushing their way onto the boat deck.

"Martha!" Seraphina cried suddenly.

"It is all right. I have already warned her," Kelvin Ward answered. "She has gone to her boat-station."

On the way out there had been boat-drill when they were passing down the Channel and again after they had reached the Mediterranean.

But Seraphina realised now that she had not the slightest idea where she had to go, and if Kelvin had not been with her she would have felt panic-stricken.

She hoped Martha would be all right, but there was no chance to think of anything but the difficulty of keeping on her feet.

The passengers who were surging up from the second-class and steerage decks were being rough as they were concerned only with reaching their own life-boats.

If Kelvin Ward had not protected her, Seraphina was certain that she would have been thrown down on the deck and trampled underfoot.

He finally managed to get her outside and they found the boat to which they had been allocated earlier in the voyage. The sailors were getting ready to let it down the side of the ship.

Some boats were already full and were only waiting for the word of command to be lowered.

It was difficult in the hurly-burly to realise what was happening, and Seraphina found it impossible to make out what anyone was saying.

"Has the Captain given orders to abandon ship?" she heard her husband ask.

No-one seemed to know the answer.

The sailors, looking anxious and turning their heads from left to right, appeared to be waiting orders from their superior Officers.

Now Seraphina was aware of the smell of smoke which appeared to be coming from the side of the ship they had just left.

"Where is the fire?" she asked and after two attempts Kelvin Ward could hear what she said.

"I think it started on the second-class deck," he shouted, "but I am not sure. No-one seems to know anything and I cannot leave you to find out."

"No . . . no of course . . . not," she said, holding on to his arm even tighter than she was doing already.

"It is all right, Seraphina," he said reassuringly. "I promise you there is no real danger."

"No . . . I am . . . sure you are . . . right," she said doubtfully.

But she was not as frightened as she thought she might be.

After all, as Kelvin had said, Bombay was only a short distance away.

The fog-horn was hooting, signals were being run up the masts and it could only be a question of time before other ships came to their rescue, if indeed they needed rescuing.

"I cannot understand how a fire at this time of the day could get a hold without anyone noticing it," she heard an elderly Englishman say angrily as he took his place beside them.

"I imagine everyone was getting ready to disembark," Kelvin Ward replied.

"I shall write to *The Times* about it," the elderly man said sharply. "This is not the sort of thing I expect to happen on a British ship."

He snorted with annoyance as he was joined by a lady shaking with terror.

"Shall we be rescued? Are you quite sure we shall be rescued?" she asked in a high, hysterical voice.

"Now, Matilda, getting yourself worked up will help no-one," her husband answered firmly.

Seraphina hoped Kelvin would not think she was behaving in the same frenzied manner.

They waited and now there seemed to be some semblance of order because most people had found their own boat-station.

It was then that Seraphina saw the Rajmata of Udaipur being wheeled by her elderly attendant and escorted by the old man, coming through the crowds towards the boat which was apparently the same as their own.

"Here is Her Highness," Seraphina said to Kelvin. "It must be worrying for her because she cannot walk and will have to be lifted into the boat."

"It will not be difficult!" he answered.

The Rajmata's chair came to a stop beside them and Seraphina moved from her husband's arm to bend towards the Princess and ask:

"Are you all right, Your Highness? My husband says there is no real danger as we are so near to Bombay."

"I am rather an encumbrance on occasions like this!" the Rajmata answered, her tone firm and unhurried.

'She is too proud to show any fear,' Seraphina told herself, 'and besides she is a Rajput!'

She felt as if a little quiver within her which had persisted despite Kelvin's soothing words was

calmer in the face of the older woman's imperturb-
ability.

Then Seraphina asked:

"The Prince . . . is he with his *Ayah*?"

"Unfortunately they have a different boat to
ours," the Rajmata replied. "One of our servants
heard of the fire almost as soon as it started and I
told the *Ayah* to go to the boat immediately."

Seraphina thought in that case the *Ayah* and
the little Prince might be in one of the boats which
were already being let down.

She leant over the railing to see one being lowered slowly on its ropes. She saw it was packed
with women and children with only enough men to
pull at the oars.

She felt a sudden quiver of fear because she
knew that when their boat was let down she would
have to go alone. Kelvin would wait with the other
men until all the women and children had got
away.

'I would like to stay with him,' Seraphina
thought to herself.

She felt a sudden terror that if he was left behind she might never see him again.

'I must ask him if I can stay,' she told herself.

But knew despairingly even as the thought
came to her he would not allow it.

It was then, still looking over the railing, that
she saw the *Ayah* who was in charge of the little
Prince. She was the only woman in the boat wearing a sari and so therefore easily distinguishable.

Seraphina was just about to turn to the
Rajmata to say that the Prince was safe because
the boat had already reached the sea when she realised the *Ayah* held nothing in her arms.

Hastily she looked at the other occupants of
the boat to see if by any chance they were holding
the Prince.

The children, and there were quite a number

of them, were all older and sitting beside the grown-ups.

There was no small child in anyone's arms!

For a moment Seraphina started wildly. Then as she turned to tell the Rajmata what had happened, she realised there was nothing the Princess could do, nor would her ancient companions be of the slightest use.

Without waiting to tell Kelvin what she was about to do she sped across the deck, entered the ship through the door by which they had left it, and hurried in the direction of the Rajmata's cabin, which was not far from their own.

Now there were no crowds to impede her, since the pushing, shoving, shouting people who had impeded their progress to the deck were all now outside.

Instead there was thick smoke, making Seraphina's eyes run and catching suffocatingly in her throat.

She fought her way through it and, reaching the suite that the Rajmata had occupied, found the door open.

She remembered from which direction the *Ayah* had brought the little Prince and pulled open the door.

As she did so she heard the child crying.

The Prince was in his cot just where his *Ayah* must have left him, too panic-stricken at the thought of the fire to remember her charge.

Seraphina snatched him up and, thinking he might find the smoke in the corridor even worse than she had, she pulled her silk shawl over her head and covered him completely.

Holding the Prince tight against her breast she hurried back the way she had come.

The smoke seemed even more blinding than it had been before and suddenly, as she moved along the corridor, flames appeared on the inside wall.

They reached out towards her and made a barrier with their red tongues.

Seraphina gave a little gasp but knew she must somehow reach Kelvin.

Only he could save them both. Only with him would she be safe.

The heat of the flames seemed about to devour her. Yet for a moment the smoke was not so thick.

"Kelvin! . . . Kelvin!" Seraphina whispered.

Then putting her face down so that she did not have to look at what lay ahead she ran forward.

She must have tightened her arms round the child until they hurt him, for she heard him scream.

Then she felt the flames scorching her hands as she passed through them.

Strong arms went round her and she heard a voice say in a tone she had never heard from him before:

"Seraphina! My God—are you all right?"

He was there! She need make no further effort!

She shut her eyes. . . .

Chapter Six

Seraphina sat on the verandah and looked out onto the garden, brilliant with flowers, and over the tree-tops to where the sea was blue beneath a faint mist which rose softly above the Bay.

Her hands, still bandaged, lay in her lap.

That morning the Doctor had said:

"There will be no need for me to call again, Mrs. Ward, unless you send for me."

"Will the scars remain for long?" Seraphina had asked.

He paused to add:

"You are a very lucky young woman, Mrs. Ward, or perhaps a very sensible one. If you had not put your shawl over your head and protected your face we might have had a very different story to tell."

Martha had said very much the same thing, except that she had added:

"If you'd not changed into your heavy silk gown, Ma'am, as I asked you to do, that muslin you're so fond of would have gone up in flames."

Seraphina was well aware that the fire might

have burnt her face and she would in fact have
been terribly scarred.

She could remember very little of what had
happened once she had passed through the flames
and felt her husband's arms go round her.

Later she had learnt that they had not even
had to leave the *Tiberius*, for the fire had been
brought under control.

While a number of the boats had got away,
she and Kelvin had remained on board and been
landed at Bombay an hour later.

"Would the Prince have been all right if I had
left him where he was?" Seraphina had asked, when
she could talk about what had happened.

"There was very considerable damage on the
second-class deck," Kelvin Ward answered, "and
several cabins on the first-class deck above where
the fire started were completely gutted—one of
them being where the Maharaj Kumar was sleeping!"

Seraphina had drawn in her breath and he
added:

"You know how brave I think you were to rescue the child as you did, but nothing I could say
can equal the gratitude of Her Highness."

The Rajmata had filled the house with flowers
and gifts, but by the time the Doctor would allow
Seraphina to see visitors, the Royal party had returned to Udaipur. So Seraphina could not receive
their thanks in person.

"I am rather glad in a way," she told Kelvin
shyly, "although I would have liked to see Her
Highness again. It is always embarrassing to be
thanked."

"You deserve their infinite gratitude," he answered. "Without you the Prince would not be
alive."

"What will happen to the *Ayah*?"

"She will be punished very severely for her
neglect of the child."

While Seraphina felt sorry for the young woman, she could not help feeling it was a dreadful action to have left the Prince in danger while she escaped to safety.

"I suppose you know you are a heroine?" Kelvin told her.

"Oh no!" Seraphina exclaimed.

"There have been headlines in the Bombay newspapers about you," he said, "and needless to say I have been besieged by journalists who wish to talk to you about what happened."

"Please . . . I cannot . . . talk about it," Seraphina cried, "and indeed there is . . . nothing to say."

"They have already said a great deal!" he answered.

"I can hardly remember what happened," Seraphina said firmly.

And that indeed was the truth.

It all seemed now like a very strange dream, and the courage that had impelled her to save the Prince melted into an overwhelming shyness at the thought of having to discuss what had happened.

Her husband managed to protect her from being troubled, and as soon as she was well enough promised to show her Bombay, which she wanted to see more than anything else.

She had learnt that his partners in the shipping company had found them the house in which they were at present living.

It was a long, low, bungalow-type mansion which had been built by a rich Parsee on the top of Malaba Hill overlooking the Bay.

It had an extensive garden and the house itself was beautifully furnished. Seraphina discovered many treasures of Indian art which delighted her, besides finding that the Indian servants with their courtesy and attention made her feel immediately at home.

What surprised her was the number of servants they needed in a comparatively small establishment, but she learnt that twenty-five was considered quite a small staff in India.

Kelvin had told her about Bombay, whose seven islands constituted a city which was different from anything else in the whole of India.

Seraphina also learnt that there were Buddhists settlers there around the third century B.C. but the first Western peoples to have taken an interest in Bombay's harbour were the Portuguese in the sixteenth century.

The beautiful Bay of Bom Bahia was acquired by Portugal, only to be given as part of her dowry to Charles II of England when in 1662 he married Catherine of Braganza, daughter of the King of Portugal.

"How fascinating!" Seraphina had exclaimed when Kelvin told her this. "I had no idea it had belonged to us for so long."

"Six years later Charles II leased it to the East India Company at a nominal rental," he answered. "But for many years the sea-routes from Bombay were menaced by pirates and sea-raiders."

"How frightening!" Seraphina exclaimed.

All the books she had read had not prepared her for the beauty of Bombay.

From the lush greenery of the Malaba Hills down to the streets surging with people, it was so brilliantly colourful.

Kelvin was able to distinguish the many different types and races, from a Jat soldier from the Punjab; a jawan; a turbanned Sikh gharri-driver with a smartly brushed beard, to a plump Marwari merchant who, he told Seraphina, would grow rich on the trade he would find for his goods in the bazaars.

On her first outing Seraphina was not allowed to do too much, but Kelvin could not resist driving her through the bazaars.

The narrow streets, overhung by tier upon tier of crazy wooden balconies, were so packed with humanity that it seemed impossible that a carriage could squeeze through them.

Jostling each other were Persian dyers, Chinese with long pigtails, Bannian shop-keepers, Arab horse-dealers from the Bendi bazaar, toddy-drawers with brass vessels on their heads, Armenian priests, Abyssinian youths and *bheestis* with their water-skins.

Besides all these everywhere were armless, legless, eyeless, half-naked beggars and large lazy Brahmini cows.

Kelvin pointed out the cotton-fluffing men twanging their string beaters and the spice-sellers proferring their colourful baskets of carmin, coriander and turmeric which he told Seraphina gave the rich gold-red colour seen in curries.

There were other traders selling cloves, nutmeg and pepper, the same spices which Vasco da Gama had carried home from India to astound the Western world in the fifteenth century.

What Seraphina loved most of all were the women in their gloriously coloured saris of red, pink, purple, green, yellow and orange, and amongst them the Moslem women modestly covered from head to foot like fat black or grey bundles.

She felt she could never see enough, but Kelvin told her laughingly there would be plenty of time for her to look at India and the Indians when she was better.

"I am well now!" she said almost petulantly. "Soon you will not be able to see the marks on my hands."

"You had a shock!" he said gently. "It takes a long time to get over shock."

Sitting now on the verandah, Seraphina thought there was a peace all round her that she had never known before.

It was like a strange happiness creeping into

her consciousness so that she could not tell how it had happened, but suddenly it was with her.

'I love India,' she told herself and knew that it was even more wonderful than she had thought it would be.

She heard a step behind her and turned her head quickly.

Kelvin was coming through the open windows onto the verandah to join her.

"How do you feel?" he asked.

"Very well, thank you. I am completely recovered. The Doctor says so and one should never argue with a Doctor!"

"Do you think you are well enough to come to a dinner-party tonight?" Kelvin Ward asked.

"But of course!" Seraphina replied. "Who has invited us?"

"It is at Parell, which is Government House," he answered. "I would like you to see it and I want you to meet the Governor, who is an old friend of mine."

"I would love that," Seraphina said.

"You are quite certain it will not be too much for you?"

"Quite certain!"

"Then I will accept!" Kelvin said. "His messenger is waiting."

He left her alone and Seraphina tried to feel excited at the thought of the dinner-party that lay ahead of her.

At the same time she knew that if she was honest she would so much rather have dined alone with her husband.

It was for her a new sort of excitement to sit opposite him in the comparatively small Dining-Room fanned by the punkahs and waited on by their white-garbed servants with coloured turbans.

She liked listening to Kelvin talking to her, explaining what he had been doing since he arrived in Bombay, and to know that he was only too willing to answer all the questions she wanted to ask him about the country and its peoples.

Nevertheless she told herself that she must make an effort to meet his friends and to like them for his sake.

She was sure, although he had never mentioned it, that he was finding it strange to come back to India and be on his own rather than with his Regiment.

'He must miss the companionship of his brother Officers,' Seraphina thought, and felt inadequate to fill the gap.

Life as far as he was concerned was completely changed. What did he really feel about it ... and her?

She wondered what gown she would wear that night and decided that if they were going to dine with the Governor Kelvin would wish her to look her best.

She decided to tell Martha she would also wear some of her jewellery.

Before she left England Sir Erasmus had given her not only the jewellery which had belonged to her mother but also as a wedding-present a diamond necklace and bracelets and the tiara in which she had been married.

Secretly Seraphina felt they were a little ostentatious; she would have preferred to wear the two strings of pearls which she remembered had been her mother's favourite jewellery.

Then she told herself she wanted Kelvin to be proud of her, and she was well aware that on her first appearance in Bombay everyone would be looking at her with curiosity.

When finally she was dressed and Martha had arranged her hair in the very latest fashion, she went a little uncertainly into the Sitting-Room where her husband was waiting for her.

The room was filled with flowers, many of

them great baskets of rare blooms from the
Rajmata.

All the windows were opened onto the verandah so that there was a vista of the flower-filled
garden and the sea beyond.

It was very lovely and Seraphina stood for a
moment in the doorway looking at her husband's
broad shoulders.

He had his back to her and she wondered what
he was thinking as he looked out onto the Bay and
seemed oblivious to his present surroundings.

She had a feeling that he was not seeing the
view, but that his thoughts were deeply concerned
with something in which she could have no part.

She suddenly felt a little afraid.

What did clothes or jewellery matter if she
could not reach him? After all, she was a stranger
in a strange land.

As if Kelvin was suddenly aware that she
stood near him he turned his head, saw her and
smiled.

"You are ready?" he asked. "I was just coming to tell you it is time that we left."

"Do I look . . . all right?"

Seraphina's eyes were on his and he saw the
anxiety in them.

Her gown was certainly very impressive. It
was Martha who had insisted that because it was
Seraphina's first appearance as a bride she should
wear white.

Ornamented with lace and satin bows, row
upon row of pleated flounces swept out behind her
like a cloud.

To hide the scars on her hands she had mit-
tens in the same soft white lace which ended at her
diamond-encircled wrists.

She wore her diamond necklace, which seemed
almost too heavy against the fragility of her neck
and skin yet somehow contrived to make her look
very young and unsure of herself.

She looked lovely, Kelvin Ward thought, and while the women would undoubtedly admire her finery, the men would want to sweep away the anxiety in her large eyes and bring a smile to the wistfulness of her lips.

"You look like a fairy Princess!" he said in his deep voice and saw her eyes light up at his words.

"You ... you do not think the diamonds are ... too much?" she enquired. "Martha insisted on my wearing them."

"This is just the right occasion for you to give them an airing!" Kelvin replied.

Seraphina smiled with the spontaneity of a child.

"That is what I am having," she said. "It is exciting going to a party with you."

"I hope you will always think so," he answered.

There was a comfortable carriage drawn by two horses with two men on the box waiting for them outside. It carried them swiftly the five miles outside Bombay where Parell is situated.

Approached by an avenue of magnificent and exotic trees a mile long, Parell with its massive walls, castellated parapets and a high red-tiled roof seemed enormous.

Arches and verandahs were lit up and rows of servants in scarlet, gold and white made it appear, Seraphina thought, like a scene at the opera.

"I wanted you to see Parell," Kelvin said, "because the Governor has decided that in the future it will not be his principal residence. Instead he will spend more time at Poona."

Inside, Seraphina found a vast Reception-Room hung with crystal chandeliers, a Banqueting-Hall eighty feet in length and the finest Ball-Room in India.

"It is like a Palace," she murmured.

They assembled in a large, white-walled Drawing-Room where they were received by

several aides-de-camp and introduced to a number
of other guests who were already there when they
arrived.

Seraphina was talking to an elderly Judge who
was telling her his own first impressions of India
when he had arrived in the country some forty
years ago, when she heard more guests being announced.

Glancing round, she drew in her breath
sharply.

Making a dramatic entrance, which Seraphina
had seen repeated and re-repeated on the *Tiberius*,
dressed in ruby red to match the jewels which decorated her dark hair and encircled her white neck,
was Lady Braithwaite.

As she swept across the room she seemed to
make every other woman pale into insignificance.

"That is Lady Braithwaite!" the Judge remarked unnecessarily. "As you may or may not
know, her husband is our G.O.C."

Seraphina managed a little murmur of assent,
which encouraged him to continue:

"I have heard tonight that Sir Reginald has
been offered the Governorship of New South
Wales. He will find it a change from India."

"Has he accepted?" Seraphina asked almost
breathlessly.

"I imagine so," the Judge answered. "It is a
great honour and will undoubtedly lead to a Peer-
age."

"How nice! How very nice for them!" Seraphina said with an enthusiasm which made the Judge
look at her in surprise.

On the opposite side of the room Lady Braithwaite was already in conversation with Kelvin
Ward, having skilfully managed to draw him a little aside from the other guests.

"You have heard that we are going to Australia?" she asked in a low, sensuous voice.

"I must congratulate you."

"We leave in ten days. I have to see you!"

He looked down into her eyes and saw an invitation that he had received before. He saw too a woman who was determined to have her own way.

"I am sure," he said quickly, "you will be far too busy packing to receive visitors."

The reply was merely a formality. It was the note in his voice that was decisive, and which said far more than words.

Lady Braithwaite's dark eyes hardened and for a moment there was an expression on her face which swept away her beauty and changed it into something ugly and venomous.

Then before she could reply Kelvin Ward turned to the nearest guest and remarked:

"We must all congratulate Sir Reginald. I am sure the Prime Minister, the Marquess of Salisbury, has made a very wise choice."

"Undoubtedly!" the man to whom he had spoken agreed courteously, "and what is our loss is Australia's gain."

At dinner Seraphina found herself on the left of the Governor while Lady Braithwaite was on his right.

As a representative of the Queen he and his wife were the last to enter the Drawing-Room and everyone stood in respectful silence while one guest after another was presented by the aides-de-camp.

"I not only want to welcome you to Bombay, Mrs. Ward," the Governor said as he greeted Seraphina, "but also to tell you how much we admired your courage in rescuing Prince Akbar. You will find that all India has opened her heart to you."

Seraphina blushed and found it impossible to reply.

Dinner was served on a verandah entirely draped with white muslin with a band playing outside in the garden.

The French Chef at Parell was renowned, and

the host of servants in their red turbans and with
the British arms emblazoned on their white tunics
was very impressive.

At dinner Seraphina found that the Governor
was a kindly man and not too difficult to talk to.

"I consider it very enterprising of your husband to embark on a new career," he said. "I feel
sure he will find it very interesting. Shipping is the
life-line of the Empire, and ships flying the Red
Ensign encircle the world."

Seraphina learnt that the Governor was an enthusiastic stamp-collector and on this subject she
was able to talk intelligently because Sir Erasmus's
collection was already spoken of as being one of
the most valuable in England.

"The mail service is amazing!" the Governor
said. "Did you know, Mrs. Ward, that the P. & O.
Company is paid nearly thirty thousand pounds a
year for carrying the Indian mails alone!"

"It seems an enormous sum!" Seraphina
agreed.

"But now the speed with which our letters
travel is even more astounding!" the Governor
went on. "Only twenty days from here to London!
Only forty days from London to Sydney! When I
was a boy, such a thing would have seemed impossible!"

"I hear, Your Excellency," the man who was
sitting on the other side of Seraphina said, "there is
a German scheme for a Berlin-to-Bagdad railway
which could considerably shorten the time to India."

"The posts are quite fast enough already, as
far as I am concerned," the Governor replied.
"Letters pour in from England every day."

"You should be in Rhodesia, as I was last
year," Seraphina's partner answered. "There the
mail is carried by runners wearing khaki shorts and
a fez. Their heavy bag weighs forty pounds and
they average a daily range of thirty miles!"

There was laughter at this and Seraphina thought she must remember to tell Kelvin what had been said, for it would undoubtedly amuse him.

She was glad to notice that he was not sitting beside Lady Braithwaite but was next to the Governor's wife and on his other side there was an elderly lady.

Seraphina guessed she was the wife of the Judge to whom she had been speaking before dinner.

When dessert had been served the Governor's wife led the ladies from the verandah and there were servants to show the way to a bed-room where they could tidy themselves before returning to the Drawing-Room.

Seraphina avoided Lady Braithwaite, but when finally they had all seated themselves and there was yet no sign of the gentlemen, Lady Braithwaite deliberately crossed the room to sit beside her.

"I have been wanting to talk to you, Mrs. Ward," she said. "There is so much I want to know about your marriage to Kelvin."

Seraphina did not reply and she went on:

"I expect he has told you what very dear and close friends we were. So I cannot help wondering why he never spoke to me of his attachment to you."

"We had not known each other ... very long," Seraphina murmured because it was obvious she had to say something.

"And of course you had something special to offer him," Lady Braithwaite said. "But what really interests me is what Kelvin is going to do with his life now that he has left the Regiment."

She smiled but there was nothing pleasant about it.

"I cannot help feeling that he will be restless without his Regimental duties to keep him interested. How do you plan to entertain him, Mrs. Ward?"

"He has an interest in a ... shipping company," Seraphina replied.

"I had not forgotten that! But do you really think Kelvin will find that enough? He has always lived such a full life and been so independent."

There was a pause before Lady Braithwaite went on:

"Of course with your money behind him there are many possibilities."

Again Lady Braithwaite appeared to wait for Seraphina to speak.

"If only that tiresome Uncle of his would die!" she continued after a moment. "With a title and money Kelvin could undoubtedly become a Governor! They are always searching for responsible people for such posts. Even the position of Viceroy is hard to fill."

Seraphina looked surprised, having always thought that to be appointed Viceroy of India must be the zenith of many men's ambitions.

"Let me let you into a little secret," Lady Braithwaite said. "It is a very expensive position and the Viceroy's allowance has to be substantially augmented from the Viceroy's private purse!"

She gave a little laugh.

"Of course that would not worry Kelvin now that he can dip his hand into yours!"

Seraphina stiffened.

She was well aware that Lady Braithwaite was being deliberately spiteful and vindictive, and she could not help praying that she would not say such things in front of Kelvin.

She could imagine only too well what his reaction would be and how angry it would make him.

Then even as she thought of him the gentlemen joined the ladies.

Kelvin instantly walked across the room to stand beside her.

Lady Braithwaite looked up at him, her dark eyes searching his face.

"I was just talking about you, Kelvin," she said. "I was telling your wife how many opportunities are open to you now that you have her fortune to assist you."

Seraphina gripped her fingers together.

She could not bear to look at her husband's face.

"At the same time," Lady Braithwaite continued, "it must be always somewhat disconcerting to have a wife who is so very much richer than one's self! How do you manage about presents, for one thing? Do you buy Mrs. Ward a birthday present with her own money, or do you give her something which cannot be bought in cash?"

She waited, then with venom in every word she finished:

"Your quite exceptional kisses for example?"

Kelvin Ward took Seraphina by the hand and drew her to her feet.

"I think," he said to her in a quiet, completely controlled voice, "that you must not do too much since this is your first night out. I am sure His Excellency will forgive us if we leave early."

With his hand under Seraphina's elbow, he moved her across the room.

It was a breach of etiquette to leave before the principal guests, who were Sir Reginald and Lady Braithwaite. But the Governor understood and excused them.

They had made their farewells and were outside and in their carriage almost before Seraphina could get her breath back.

'How could Lady Braithwaite have said such things?' she asked herself as they drove in silence.

She knew Kelvin was angry—so angry that she could feel it exuding from him like the vibrations from an electric machine.

There was nothing she could say.

She only knew that Lady Braithwaite had avenged herself in a subtle and effective manner and had wounded Kelvin with every word she'd uttered.

It had touched him on the raw, but there was nothing Seraphina could do that would ease his hurt.

Money! Her money!

Those thousands of golden pounds which stood like a barrier between them and which she knew were a humiliation which struck at his pride every time he was reminded of them.

Vaguely she realised that Lady Braithwaite was striking at Kelvin because she herself had been hurt. He must, Seraphina thought, have antagonised her in some exceptional way to arouse her to such a pitch of malignance.

Yet she could feel no triumph or satisfaction in the thought, because Lady Braithwaite's revenge had been so swift and deliberate.

'I hate her! I hate her!' Seraphina told herself.

But she knew hopelessly that there was nothing she could do to make things better, and anything she might say could bring down upon her own head the fury she felt was seething in her husband.

When they reached their house Seraphina walked in ahead, wishing she were older and knew what to do.

Someone who was sophisticated and experienced in the handling of men, like Lady Braithwaite, would know the right attitude for a situation such as this.

Seraphina felt young, gauche and utterly inadequate to cope with anything but her own apprehension and horror at what had been said.

In the Sitting-Room there was a tray of drinks laid on a table and several letters which must have come late in the evening.

She crossed the room.

"I . . . I think . . . I will . . . go to bed," she said, hoping as she spoke that Kelvin would ask her to stay.

"I expect you are tired," he replied, speaking for the first time since they had left Parell. "Good-night."

"Good-night," Seraphina said forlornly.

She went out through the inner door which led to the small Hall from which opened the main bed-rooms.

Kelvin's and hers had a communicating door. It was tightly closed—and likely to remain so, Seraphina thought.

She knew how hurt and angry he was, but she wished he would come in and talk to her about how he felt. If he did perhaps they could laugh at it together and then it would cease to be so important.

She knew such an idea was impossible.

Her room had been shut up for the night, but she pulled back the curtains from the windows.

She opened not only the long casements which led onto the verandah, but also the outer windows of close network.

It was still too cool at night for there to be any necessity for sleeping under mosquito netting.

Seraphina felt the night air soft and moist on her bare neck and arms.

The stars glittered in an enormous sky and she could hear the chip-chip of the grasshoppers on the lawn.

'It is so beautiful. We ought to be happy,' she told herself.

Yet for the moment Lady Braithwaite had destroyed the peace and happiness she had felt that afternoon and the closeness she had known with Kelvin ever since they had arrived in Bombay.

"I hate her! I hate her! I hate her!" Seraphina said over and over again.

She had told Martha not to wait up for her.

The maid was getting old, and although it was not yet really hot in the daytime she found it oppressive. Seraphina was sure that Kelvin was right. It would be best for her to return to England.

She undid her gown without much difficulty, hung it up in the wardrobe and then took off her other clothes.

Martha had left a night-gown ready on a chair, which she picked up and slipped over her head.

It was of the finest lawn with inserts of lace; Seraphina knew that only her father would have known that lawn was the right night attire for the heat and that no type of silk was suitable for Indian weather.

'Papa's eye to detail is fantastic!' she thought and knew this was another matter which would annoy Kelvin if he were aware of it.

It was, however, a very remote possibility, she thought with a feeling almost of despair, that he would ever know what she wore at night.

She wondered if she should brush her hair and then decided that as Martha had brushed it thoroughly before she had arranged it for the dinner-party, it would not be necessary.

Instead she pulled out the pins and let it fall over her shoulders.

Then she blew out the candles on the dressing-table.

She had not used the electric light with which the house was fitted because when she entered the room she had wanted to look at the stars.

She also knew that the light would attract moths.

There were in fact a number of them already circling round the single candle left burning by the side of the bed.

Seraphina thought that now she must close the curtains otherwise she would be awakened by the early morning light.

Dawn came at about four o'clock and she must sleep later than that, otherwise she would have a very long time to wait before she saw Kelvin at breakfast time.

'What is he feeling? What is he thinking?' she asked herself.

She had a sudden longing to open the communicating door and go into his bed-room.

She listened. She thought that a few seconds before she had heard a movement.

She had not been mistaken. There was another sound, only a faint one, and she knew he was in his bed-room.

He will still be angry, she thought despairingly, hating her money and perhaps her too.

She thought of what they would have to endure for the rest of their married life!

Even if people were not so outspoken or so spiteful as Lady Braithwaite had been, there would always be those who would insinuate or, worse still, Kelvin would think they were doing so that he was dependent upon his wife.

Seraphina shut her eyes.

She felt completely and utterly inadequate to cope either with the present or with the future.

She wanted more than anything in her whole life for her husband to be happy, and yet she knew there would be no happiness if they were always to be over-shadowed by the size of her immense fortune.

'Why can I not give him all my money?' she asked herself.

Then knew that this too would be impracticable.

He would not accept it, and anyway the situation would hardly change. As it was he had the use of everything she possessed.

If he wished to write out a cheque there was nothing she could do to prevent it, nor could her

father, if it came to that, since he had been given
complete control of his wife's wealth.

'There must be some solution,' Seraphina
thought desperately.

But if there was she could not think of it.

'I must go to bed,' she told herself.

She opened her eyes. Then as she took a step
forward she stood transfixed.

Coming in through the open window, slither-
ing over the lintel, was a snake!

She stared at it panic-stricken and without really realising what she was doing she climbed up on
the arm-chair from which she had taken her night-
gown.

The snake in the flickering candle-light seemed
to be advancing towards her.

She stood for a moment watching it, feeling it
was impossible to articulate until hoarsely so that
the first word was only a croak she called out:

"Kelvin! Kelvin!"

The snake seemed to check for a moment at
the sound of her voice and raised its head.

Then as she thought Kelvin could not have
heard her she tried to cry out again, but her voice
was strangled in her throat.

He opened the door.

"Did you call, Seraphina?"

She could not answer.

She tried to speak but no sound would come.

"What is it?" he asked.

He came into the room and looked surprised
to see her standing on the chair.

He followed the direction of her eyes and saw
the snake on the floor.

Instantly his hand went to his side where if he
had been in uniform his revolver would have been.
Then as if he suddenly realised he was wearing only
his shirt and trousers, he said sharply:

"Stay where you are! Do not move!" and
went back into his bed-room.

Seraphina could not have moved even if she had tried.

She felt as if she had been turned to stone.

She could only hold her breath, waiting, feeling that it was a race between Kelvin's return and the snake reaching her.

But even as he came back through the door, his revolver in his hand, the snake turned and with incredible swiftness slithered back the way it had come out through the window and across the verandah, and disappeared into the garden.

Kelvin followed it across the room but by the time he reached the verandah there was no sign of it.

"You should not have opened the outer window," he began as he turned back.

He saw that Seraphina was still standing on the chair and knew by her face that she was terrified.

He went to her and, putting his arms round her, lifted her down onto the floor.

"It is all right, Seraphina," he said gently. "The snake has gone. I do not think it was a dangerous one but a Coluber which is comparatively harmless."

She made an inarticulate little sound and clung to him, burying her face against his shoulder.

He could feel her trembling and remembered that this was how she had trembled on their wedding-night when she had waited for him to come to her bed-room.

He held her close and went on speaking in a quiet, calm voice.

"It is my fault. I should have warned you not to open the outer window at night. It lets in the air but prevents birds, lizards and bats from coming into the house. Wild creatures in India are insatiably curious. I once found a whole family of monkeys encamped on my bed!"

He thought that Seraphina was listening and was not trembling so violently.

But he could feel that her soft, warm body beneath the thin lawn of her night-gown was still tense and her face was pressed hard against his shoulder.

There was the same sweet Spring fragrance from her hair that he had noticed in her cabin the night before the fire.

"I am sorry that should have happened tonight," he went on. "You looked well and so pretty when we set out for Parell and I wanted you to enjoy yourself."

"The . . . snake . . . was like . . . her!" Seraphina murmured in a voice so low that he could hardly hear it.

He did not pretend not to understand of whom she was speaking.

"But they are neither of them as venomous or as dangerous as they appear," he answered quietly.

He felt that his words surprised Seraphina and for a moment she no longer trembled.

"I am going to carry you to bed," he said gently. "I think you would rather not walk on the floor and I want you to rest. You have had enough excitement for one night."

She did not protest and he picked her up in his arms.

She was very light. He carried her across the room and she laid her head against his shoulder like a child.

He set her very gently down on the big bed which had been turned down by the servants.

Then he pulled the sheet over Seraphina and sat down facing her.

She looked as she had the night of their wedding, very small and fragile against the white pillows, her fair hair framing her frightened eyes.

She seemed, as she had then, little more than a child.

"How could I imagine that anyone as small as you could become involved in so many dramatic and unfortunate episodes?" he asked.

He smiled as he spoke and, as if he had magnetised her, Seraphina found herself attempting a warm little smile.

"I am . . . sorry to be . . . such a . . . nuisance."

"You are, as you well know, nothing of the sort," Kelvin Ward replied, "but if you give me many more shocks I shall have a heart-attack!"

"I . . . I am frightened of . . . snakes."

"So am I!" Kelvin answered. "It is only the most holy type of Yogi who can treat them as a brother and who will not kill them. Neither will the snakes harm him."

"Are there . . . holy men like that?"

"A few."

"Oh . . . I would like to . . . meet one!"

"You shall," he replied, "and now I am going to tell you something which I think will please you."

"What is . . . it?"

He noticed there was still some apprehension in her eyes, but he knew she was making a tremendous effort at self-control.

"I found when we got back tonight an invitation from the Maharana of Udaipur," Kelvin answered. "I will not read his letter to you now because it would take too long and I want you to go to sleep, but he expresses his gratitude in the most gracious terms and asks if we will pay him a visit. Would you like to go to Udaipur?"

"Could we?"

The apprehension was gone. Now there was only excitement in the blue eyes and without realising that she was doing so Seraphina's hand went out towards him.

He took her fingers in his.

"If you promise that you will not be upset by the journey and that you will not fall off an elephant's back or be eaten by a crocodile, I will take you."

"How wonderful! I promise so when can we go?"

"The day after tomorrow if it pleases you—if you can be ready by then."

"I am ready now . . . this moment!"

He laughed.

"You must give me a little more time to make arrangements."

"The day after tomorrow?" she asked.

"It is a deal!"

Her fingers tightened on his.

"You will be able to show me India . . . at least some of it."

"And a very beautiful part," he answered. "But now you must go to sleep."

He looked down at the hand that he held, the skin still scarred from the flames.

Seraphina tried to take her hand away.

"It is so . . . ugly!" she murmured.

"They are decorations for bravery," Kelvin said quietly.

Then very gently he turned her hand over in his and kissed her palm.

Chapter Seven

"This must be the loveliest place in the world!" Seraphina said aloud.

"I agree!" Kelvin answered.

They were standing in a window of the Palace on the Lake called Jugnewas and looking at the Maharana of Udaipur's Palace on the other side of the water.

A building of white granite and marble rising at least one hundred feet from the ground, the Palace was flanked with octagonal towers and crowned with cupolas.

It stood on the very edge of the lake but elevated above it so that its reflection shimmered on the water beneath it, while other Palaces stretched away into the distance to where the encircling green hills rose against the blue sky.

It was so lovely, so breathtaking, that Seraphina felt as if she had entered a strange fairy-land which until now had existed only in her imagination.

But then everything had seemed enchanted

from the moment they'd left Bombay and set out
on their journey North.

First there had been the excitement of
boarding the train at the Victoria Terminus in
Bombay.

Seraphina had travelled quite a lot in her life,
but she had never imagined anything could be so
fantastic as an Indian Railway Station.

The Station itself, as Kelvin had explained
with a twinkle in his eyes, was a monument to the
English imagination.

Seraphina looked at him in surprise and he
went on:

"In Indian cities the grandest and the most
ornamental buildings are often the Railway Stations, and in designing them the architects have really run riot."

He laughed.

"They are like a giant's mock Oriental cara-
vanserais, all domes, clocks, stained-glass windows,
whirlygigs and immense glass and girder roofs, all
designed to cosset the magic metal railway lines."

Seraphina laughed, but when she saw Bombay
Station she realised he had not exaggerated.

Besides the theatrical background there was
the usual frantic confusion of Indian travellers.

There were Indians in saris, dhotis, torn rags
and turbans, in baggy white shorts, scarlet uni-
forms, yellow priestly robes, bush-jackets and
loin-cloths.

There were hawkers shouting in hollow voices,
office-messengers skurrying to post their letters in
the mail-coach box and bleating goats being led to
the guard's van.

Besides these there were entire families sitting,
eating, feeding babies, sleeping on piles of luggage
and screaming whenever a train steamed and hissed
into the Station.

'Like a fire-breathing dragon,' Seraphina
thought.

When finally the great Indian Peninsula Railway carried them North to Khandwa, the Stations at which they stopped en route were to Seraphina an unending source of amusement and interest.

Apparently not only the travellers who, Kelvin told her, always arrived days before the actual date of their journey to camp on the platform, but goats, chickens, pai-dogs and pigeons seemed to live on the Station, and very often there was a sacred bull!

Indian traders were not likely to miss an opportunity of making money and the travellers were an unfailing source of business.

There were sellers of curry and savoury hot food; sweet-sellers who also provided sherbet; and coconut-sellers with a special knife to cut off the top of the green coconut so that the customer could drink the cool milk.

Water-sellers were everywhere, their skins filled with different water for Moslems and Hindus.

"That is the Chai-wallah," Kelvin said to Seraphina, pointing to a tea-seller moving up and down the platform with his cry of "Garam-chai," which she realised meant 'hot tea.'

At every Station all the passengers on the train left it to wash, to buy food or merely to stretch their legs.

Then when it was time for them to return to the train there was such a violent shouting, crying and blowing of whistles that everyone became panic-stricken in case they were left behind.

Seraphina found that Kelvin had booked two compartments for themselves and others for his servants.

She was astonished to find how many servants were necessary to accompany them on the journey.

She had said good-bye to Martha at Bombay, and although the elderly woman wept a tear or two, Seraphina knew that she was glad to be returning to the comfort and security of England.

"I have not had time to find you an Indian maid," Kelvin told Seraphina, "but instead I am providing you with a personal servant in the shape of Amar. He had told me that he has been trained by an English Mem-Sahib to be what is to all intents and purposes a lady's-maid."

"A man?" Seraphina asked.

"It is very usual out here, I assure you," Kelvin answered. "Amar tells me that he is used to looking after a lady's clothes besides being a *dhirzi*."

"What is that?" Seraphina asked.

"A tailor," Kelvin replied. "It means he can not only mend everything for you but can even make you some dresses if you want him to do so."

"He sounds excellent!" Seraphina exclaimed.

When she met Amar she liked him at once.

He was a small man of middle age who moved quietly and appeared to have an artistic appreciation of beautiful gowns and the handling of them.

She was soon to find she had only to tell him something once for him never to forget it, and in innumerable ways he saw to her comfort in a manner that Martha had never been able to do.

When it was time to go to sleep on the train, their beds were made up with their own sheets, pillows and even their own mats on which to put their feet.

In the morning, after breakfast had been brought to their carriages, everything was tidied away again as if by magic before the train moved on.

Seraphina enjoyed the food which was provided by Kelvin telegraphing his requirements ahead.

As the train drew into a Station, out of the shadows would appear a man in white carrying their meal, whatever it might be, on a tray covered by a napkin.

There were fiery curries with chutneys and onions and chupattis, together with whisky and cool bottles of soda water for Kelvin and fresh lime-juice for her.

When they stopped at an unimportant Station they had to eat quickly because before they left the man in white would want his plates back again.

Sometimes as the train moved off slowly with a creaking of its woodwork and chuffing of its engine, he would run beside it still calling out for a plate, spoon, cup or whatever was being carried away!

There was so much to see and so much to do that the two nights and days on the train seemed to pass more quickly than Seraphina would have believed possible.

At Khandwa they transferred to the Rajputana-Malwa line and proceeded via Indore and Nimach to Chitorgarh.

"Now we become the guests of His Highness," Kelvin said with a smile as they drew into the Station, "and I think you will find that you are a very important visitor and will be treated like Royalty."

That was certainly true!

Seraphina found waiting for them at the Station not only a carriage drawn by four white horses but resplendent members of the Maharana's private Army carrying lances with colourful pennants.

They set off in style and now Seraphina could see the country which she had longed to visit and realised that they had not exaggerated when they had told her that Rajputan was romantic.

There were hills, rock plateaus, and bare cliffs springing out of fertile plains. There were massive forts and picturesque palaces.

Wild birds and yellow cactus hedges in flower were a delight to the eyes. Seraphina was thrilled to see many camels besides the lazy, patient-eyed buffalos and occasionally an elephant.

The Rajasthan women looked like birds of paradise.

Instead of saris they wore a full pleated usually red skirt just above their ankles, a contrasting bodice often peacock blue and a *orhni* or mantle perhaps in orange.

And every woman, even those working on the roads, was festooned with silver anklets, bracelets, amulets, necklaces and charms.

Each movement was a rhythmic orchestration!

There was so much to exclaim about, so many questions to ask!

It was only later that night that Seraphina began to wonder if perhaps Kelvin had found her too child-like in her enthusiasm.

They stayed the first night at a small Palace belonging, they learnt, to a minor Maharaja who was a relation of their host.

Everything was done to make them comfortable, but Seraphina found it impossible to talk to Kelvin alone. Actually after the journey she was glad to go to bed early.

The next day followed much the same pattern as the first. She learnt they were drawing near to Udaipur and could in fact have reached it that night had not the Maharana wished to receive them in State.

"Put on one of your prettiest gowns," Kelvin advised her before they retired to bed. "Tomorrow is very important."

"For you?" she asked.

"Not at all," he answered. "It is you who are the real guest of honour, the person to whom they are really grateful."

"I hope they will not say . . . too much," Seraphina said shyly.

"You have only to smile and look beautiful," he replied. "I will do all the talking that is necessary."

There was something protective and comforting about the way he spoke, and when she was in bed Seraphina found she was unable to sleep because her thoughts were of him.

She was so relieved to get away from Bombay and Lady Braithwaite that she had hardly been able to think of anything else.

But she could not forget the manner in which he had kissed her hand!

It had been a gesture, she told herself, that he might have made to anyone, and yet she had known that at the touch of his lips something strange and unexpected had happened within herself.

It was as if a tiny flame awoke and flickered inside her. It made her quiver . . . but not with fear.

His lips had only touched her skin for a second and yet when he released her hand she felt as if she must hold on to him, as if she could not let him go!

Then she told herself he was only being kind.

She had been frightened and upset both by Lady Braithwaite and the snake. He had been as reassuring and comforting as he had been on their wedding-night and when she had been frightened by the storm.

'But I really mean nothing to him!' she told herself. 'I am just a woman with whom he was forced into marriage!"

She wondered why the thought seemed to hurt her more than it had at any other time since they had been married.

She thought perhaps it was only because she was frightened of the damage Lady Braithwaite could do to the friendship growing between herself and Kelvin.

Yet this fear appeared to make her more apprehensive and more vulnerable than she had ever been before.

Every mile of their journey towards Udaipur

Seraphina thought how thankful she was to escape from Bombay.

Now there was no reason to worry that Lady Braithwaite and Kelvin might be seeing each other, or that once again she might have to endure the spite and venom with which the older woman had referred to her money.

'When we get back she will have gone!' Seraphina told herself with satisfaction.

Once again she remembered the feel of Kelvin's lips firm and warm against her palm.

As they approached the outskirts of Udaipur they were met by soldiers on horse-back who led them through the town until suddenly just ahead of them they saw the Palace silhouetted against the sky.

Soldiers guarded the main entrance and as they alighted from the carriage the Bukshee—Commander of the Maharana's forces—came forward to greet them.

He was flanked by the Royal Insignia, the Standard and kettle-drums.

Behind him there were nobles and important members of the Government who led Seraphina and Kelvin through soldiers standing at attention towards the Great Hall of Assembly.

On their way they passed through a number of Saloons each filled with spectators: women in saris, turbanned men wearing their decorations who all stood as they passed.

Seraphina longed to put her hand into her husband's, but she felt it would look undignified and instead, with a shy smile on her face, she gracefully moved beside him.

Suddenly she heard a herald's voice announce to 'The Lord of the World' that his guests had arrived!

In the Great Hall, which Seraphina learnt later was known as Surya Mahi—'Hall of the

Sun'—there was a huge medallion depicting the sun in splendour which was the arms of the Maharana.

Beneath it was the *Gadi*, or throne, under a velvet canopy supported on silver columns.

The throne was only a huge cushion, as Seraphina had learnt was usual in the East, but over it was thrown a velvet mantle embroidered with gold and precious stones.

The Maharana rose as they approached and she saw that he was a magnificent-looking man and was glad that he did not disappoint her expectations.

His Highness Maharana Dhiraj Fateh Singh Bahadur was nearly forty and his beard, already streaked with grey, was parted in the centre and swept sideways and upwards to give him a very distinctive and unusual appearance.

He greeted both Seraphina and Kelvin with the traditional *Namaskar* and made a short speech in which he thanked Seraphina for saving the life of his son and bade them welcome on behalf of all his people.

Kelvin answered him and then they sat down surrounded by the nobles and dignitaries of the Palace.

Gifts were presented which Kelvin had already warned Seraphina she must be ready to accept.

For her there was an exquisite necklace of pearls with a huge pendant set with rubies and diamonds in the front and wrought behind with the delicate enamel-work which she knew was one of the great crafts of India.

There were the matching ear-rings and bracelets to accompany the necklace, and besides this there were shawls and brocades all in the most exquisite colours and many of them embroidered with real jewels.

Kelvin was told that for him there were two horses with silver and gilt bridles.

"But these," the Maharana smiled, "you will see tomorrow."

When the more formal part of the Reception was over they moved into a smaller Saloon where the Rajmata was waiting for them and beside her the Maharanee and the little Prince.

"I am so delighted to be here, Your Highness," Seraphina said when she greeted them.

"We are very proud that you accepted our invitation," the Rajmata answered.

Kelvin had also provided gifts which Seraphina had not seen until they were brought forward by one of the servants and placed on a side-table.

There was a large silver rose-bowl for the Rajmata, a silver box for the Maharana, a cut-glass scent-bottle for his wife, and for Prince Akbar a number of English toys.

Seraphina knew it was because he had not wished to trouble her that Kelvin had chosen these himself, and she was surprised at how clever he had been in buying toys which were exactly right for a small boy of two years old.

They talked with the Rajmata for some time and were then joined by the Maharana.

Everything was quite informal until it was suggested that Seraphina and her husband might wish to rest before the banquet which was being given in their honour that evening.

It was then they learnt that the Maharana had put at their disposal the Palace on the Lake.

"I told His Highness," the Rajmata said, "that you have only just been married and I could not think of anywhere that would be more appropriate for what you call a honeymoon than the Lake Palace."

At first Seraphina did not realise what she meant, but when they left the Maharana's Palace and went outside she saw in the centre of the lake there was a delicate fairy-like building shimmering in the sunshine and reflected in the water beneath it.

"That is the Lake Palace," said the Purdhan, or Prime Minister, who was escorting them.

There was a barge rowed by ten oarsmen to take them across the lake to the Palace and when Seraphina saw it she knew why the Rajmata had suggested it would be perfect for a honeymoon.

Made of white marble, its columns, reservoirs, fountains and walls were inlaid with mosaics and the apartments were decorated with historical paintings in water colours.

There were parterres of flowers and orange and lemon groves in the centre of the buildings shaded by the wide-spreading tamarand and evergreen kheenee, while the palmyra waved plume-like branches over the dark cyprus.

"This Palace was built," the Purdhan said, "for the Chiefs so that they could rest here after their wars and hear only the songs of love."

The whole Palace covered about four acres, and yet as it had been given over to them Seraphina felt it had a quiet intimacy that was not in any way awe-inspiring.

Everything was a delight, from the purple and crimson beauty of the flowers to the gold and yellow of the orange groves.

It was only when she went up into the big bed-room where she would sleep alone that she wished there were songs of love for her and Kelvin within the marble walls of Jugnewás.

But at first there was little time to think.

She had to rest and change for what she knew was to be a very important banquet in their honour.

She chose a gown of pale pink tulle on which glittered tiny diamenté like dew-drops before the morning sun has dispersed them.

Yet even with her diamond necklace and the diamonds arranged skillfully in her hair by Amar, she felt it would be impossible for her to compete with the beauty of the Indian women in their saris or the magnificent jewels worn by the Maharanee and the other ladies at the banquet.

Seraphina had learnt that the Rajput Princesses did not cover their faces in public like many other Indian women did.

Nevertheless, out of respect for the Maharana and because an Indian woman is always supposed to be beautiful and must therefore not reveal that she grows old, they held their saris sideways across their faces.

But they laughed and talked and their conversation was as intelligent and well informed as that of the men.

Course succeeded course and there were many strange and exotic dishes besides the delicious curries which Seraphina had learnt to enjoy and appreciate.

As soon as the banquet was over they were able to leave and once again were rowed back to the Lake Palace.

"It has been a tiring day," Kelvin said when at last those who had accompanied them bowed themselves away and there was only the sound of the oars splashing gently in the water as they disappeared.

"I am a little weary," Seraphina answered.

"Then go to bed," he advised, "and do not hurry up in the morning. I shall be leaving very early. I am going on a tiger-shoot."

"A tiger-shoot!" Seraphina exclaimed.

"The Maharana is very anxious for me to shoot one which has been terrorising the villagers for some time. I think however he has been deftly preserving it for my arrival, and I only hope I do not disgrace myself by missing it."

"I am sure you are a very good shot," Seraphina smiled.

He did not contradict her and then a little wistfully she said:

"What time do you think you will be back to-morrow?"

"You will not be lonely," he replied. "The Rajmata has plans to entertain you, and I know that you will be happy in her company."

"Yes, of course," Seraphina agreed hastily.

"And tomorrow night," Kelvin said, "there is to be Indian dancing which I am sure you will enjoy. I believe the dancing we shall see in Udaipur is very exceptional."

"I would like that."

"Then sleep well, Seraphina."

She waited a moment, hoping that he might kiss her hand as he had done in Bombay, but he only smiled at her and she turned away and found a servant waiting to escort her up the marble stairs and along the balcony to her bed-chamber.

There was the sweet scent of jasmine and the exotic fragrance of the lotus flowers which covered much of the lake.

When Seraphina entered her own room and looked out of the window she saw the moon shimmering on the water and turning it to silver.

The cupolas and towers of the Palace were dark against the star-lit sky and in her imagination she could hear songs of love coming across the water.

"A Palace for a honeymoon!" she whispered.

Then feeling very lonely she crept into bed.

The morning brought sunshine and in the beauty of the Lake Palace it was impossible, Seraphina told herself, to be anything but happy.

More gifts were brought to her, so many of them that she felt embarrassed by the very small and unimportant presents she and Kelvin had brought with them.

There were shawls, brocades, muslins and jewels from the noblemen and officials who, like the Maharana, were grateful to her for saving the life of the Maharaj Kumar.

Fortunately she had a number of small wed-

ding-gifts in her luggage which Kelvin had suggested they should bring with them to Udaipur.

Out of them Seraphina chose an attractive
hand-mirror set with a design in turquoises, a stone
which she knew was considered to be lucky in the
East.

Amar packed it up in white paper, found a red
ribbon with which to tie it and Seraphina carried it
with her when the barge took her across the lake to
the Palace.

From the Rajmata's apartments she could see
the Lake Palace like a translucent pearl mirrored in
the silver water.

When approaching the Princess's apartments
Seraphina had realised there were other rooms
leading off the long, narrow passages from which
came the sound of gay, feminine voices, the twang
of a sitar and sometimes someone singing.

These she knew belonged to the ladies who
lived in the Maharana's Palace, but she was not
quite certain what their position was in the household.

It was impossible either when she arrived or at
the banquet last night to speak alone with the Maharanee but now she found her waiting in the
Rajmata's apartments. She was not only beautiful
but very young.

Kelvin had told her the Maharana's age and it
seemed strange that he should have such a very
young wife until she learnt that he had married the
present Maharanee only three years ago.

Very slim and beautiful as must have been the
Rajmata in the past, it was obvious that the Maharanee was very shy.

Having talked to Seraphina for only a short
while in a somewhat stilted manner, she left her
mother-in-law's apartments taking the baby Prince
with her.

"Her Highness is very lovely," Seraphina said
to the Rajmata.

"She is not yet at her ease with English ladies because she sees so few," the Rajmata replied. "She asked me to express to you all the words she finds it difficult to say—her deep and undying gratitude that you saved her son's life."

"I want no more thanks, Your Highness," Seraphina protested. "You have all been far too generous and it is embarrassing to have so many wonderful things said to me and receive so many extravagant presents."

"How can one ever re-pay the gift of a life?" the Rajmata asked.

"I can understand what Her Highness feels about Prince Akbar," Seraphina said. "He is such a dear little boy."

"His Highness is very proud of him," the Rajmata replied.

"His Highness had no son by his first marriage?"

The Rajmata shook her head.

"It was a great sadness," she said. "My son was married when he was fourteen and while there were several girl children of the marriage there was no son."

"But now he has an heir," Seraphina exclaimed with satisfaction. "Is Her Highness a Rajput Princess?"

"Yes indeed," the Rajmata answered. "Her father is the Maharaja of a Province not far from here."

"Oh! They met each other and fell in love!" Seraphina cried romantically.

The Rajmata smiled.

"A Hindu bride does not see her husband before the marriage," she replied. "The wedding is arranged because they are both suitable for each other and the signs are auspicious."

Seraphina was silent.

There was so much difference in the ages of the young Maharanee and her husband and she

knew how the Maharanee must have felt leaving
her father's home to marry a man she had never
seen.

She realised the Rajmata was watching her
and there was a kindly expression in the elderly
woman's eyes.

"It may seem strange to you, Mrs. Ward," she
said, "that our people do not fall in love as you
know it until after the marriage, but the women
know that they will love their husbands."

"How can they know that?" Seraphina asked.
"And surely they must be . . . . frightened?"

She was thinking of herself as she spoke. She
had no idea how expressive her face was as she
remembered her own fear on her wedding-night,
and how large and over-powering Kelvin had
seemed when he came into her bed-room.

"A Hindu woman," the Rajmata said gently,
"worships life as the divine fire, and her bridegroom is the personification of Krishna, the god of
Love."

Seraphina's eyes were on her face as the old
Princess went on:

"Love begets life, and therefore when two people are joined by the divine fire they too become
gods."

There was silence. Then Seraphina knelt down
beside the Rajmata's chair.

"Explain to me, please," she begged, "tell me,
Your Highness, so that I can understand what love
means between a man and . . . a woman so that . . .
a bride will love her husband and not be . . .
afraid."

The moon was high in the Heavens and its silver light made the Lake Palace look as if it were
about to float away into the star-lit sky.

Ringing in Seraphina's ears was the music to
which they had been listening in the Palace and it
seemed to her as if for the first time in her life she

had understood what dancing should mean and what it expressed.

In honour of the occasion the dances and the music had been part of the work of Kalidasa, the master poet and dramatist who had lived in 390 A.D. They told in mime, song and dance the story of how once Spring had failed to come to India.

The gods were beset by the anguished prayers of men for cold weather or hot weather, for rain and above all the fertility of the absent Spring.

The gods therefore deputed Krishna, god of Love, to try to put things right, and he journeyed deep into the Himalayas taking with him his wife, Rati—or Desire.

Everywhere they went Krishna awoke the animals to love.

Two lines of the poem translated into English remained in Seraphina's mind:

*The forest creatures showed the passion springing
In every bridegroom's heart towards his bride . . .*

She found herself repeating it beneath her breath as the boat pushing aside the lotus blossoms moved through the still water until they reached the landing-stage at the Lake Palace.

She knew now as she had known ever since she talked to the Rajmata that all she had felt for Kelvin and the strange fire that had been lit within her when he kissed her palm was—love!

She could not imagine now how she had ever believed that what she felt for him was friendship.

She must have loved him from the moment when they had made their pact the night of their marriage and when he had been so kind to her during the voyage!

Most of all she had loved him with an agonised jealousy when she had heard Lady Braithwaite describing him as an "alluring, attractive, passionate lover."

'I love him! I love him!' Seraphina told herself, 'but I did not recognise it until now.'

She had not expected love to be a pain within her breast or a constriction in her throat, a longing to be beside a man—not necessarily to talk to him or to touch him, but content because he was there.

Yet when they had driven back from Parell and she had known how angry he was, it was love that had made her feel as if Lady Braithwaite had driven a dozen daggers into her heart.

It was love that had made her think that both Lady Braithwaite and the snake were menacing her, trying to destroy something miraculous and wonderful rising within her very soul.

She asked herself now how she could have been so stupid as to have been afraid of Kelvin so that she had prevented him from becoming her bride-groom.

"I want him to love me!" she told herself.

Then she knew that the song was wrong. There was "no passion springing" in Kelvin's heart towards his bride. He had said himself that he did not wish to marry her.

How could he possibly want a tiresome, frightened, innocent girl who had been thrust upon him when he preferred sophisticated women?

Yet from what the Rajmata had told her, Seraphina knew that a man and woman who had never met before could come to love each other.

At the dancing that night she had watched the Maharana and his wife. She had seen a sudden softening in the magnificent Ruler's expression when his eyes rested on the downcast face of his wife.

Shimmering in a sari embroidered with diamonds, she had looked exquisitely lovely but very young.

She was in fact only seventeen—a year younger than Seraphina—and yet she had been married for three years and had given her husband a son.

'He loves her!' Seraphina thought, 'yet when she became his wife he had no idea what she looked like.'

But she had loved him and worshipped him because he was Krishna—because he was to her divine even as the god himself was divine.

'That is what I feel for Kelvin,' Seraphina told herself.

Again she felt that little quiver of fire at the thought that she could be his wife and he would come to love her even as the Maharana loved his young bride.

Seraphina had known when she had gone back from the Palace after being with the Rajmata that she was no longer afraid.

Now she understood! Now that it had been explained to her what love meant between a man and a woman she no longer trembled at the thought of it.

'Why did nobody tell me?' she asked herself. 'Yet Indian girls understand such things almost as soon as they begin to talk.'

'It is ignorance that arouses fear!' Seraphina thought, 'not knowledge.'

It was what many people had discovered before her, but to her it was a revelation!

"I am no longer afraid!" she wanted to cry to the stars and felt her heart singing with the joy of it.

Then as they stepped out onto the cool marble stage from the barge she realised that Kelvin and she were alone and she knew that she had to make him understand.

They walked together into the big comfortable Salon which overlooked the lake.

The servants brought them cool drinks and withdrew.

Kelvin seated himself in a deep arm-chair and Seraphina thought as she glanced at him how handsome, how irresistibly attractive he looked.

It was, she thought, perhaps the masculinity of him which had frightened her at first, but now it had a very different effect upon her.

He was so much a man that she could understand why women were attracted by him; why they wanted him and why they could not bear to lose him.

'But I am his wife!' she told herself proudly.

Again she found the words of the song ringing in her ears: ". . . *with passion springing.*"

Did Kelvin feel any passion for her? Could she make him?

If the Rajmata was to be believed, a man naturally felt passion for a beautiful woman and inevitably for his wife.

But the Rajmata was speaking of Indian men. Would it be the same for Kelvin?

He was so controlled, and yet every time he had been angry she had been acutely aware of it. She had felt the vibrations of it exuding from him, frightening her with its intensity.

Would she not have known if he had felt any different emotion where she was concerned?

The elation and freedom she had felt when she left the Rajmata began to fade a little.

It was one thing to tell herself that she loved her husband and she would make him love her, but quite a different thing to translate it into words and . . . actions.

Supposing he still actively disliked her as he had on their wedding-night?

Without realising what she was doing, Seraphina rose to put her glass down on the table and walk towards the open window.

The beauty and enchantment of the lake was like a mirage of dreams in front of her.

'I must make him . . . understand! I must tell him that I am no longer . . . afraid!' she whispered in her heart.

It seemed to her as if Krishna, the god of

Love, with his beautiful liquid eyes was near her, telling her what to say.

"Kelvin . . ." she began in a voice which unexpectedly trembled.

He looked across the room at her seeing her slender figure silhouetted against the darkness, the diamanté on her tulle gown shimmering in the moonlight.

"Yes?" he questioned.

"I . . . I have . . . something to . . . tell you." Seraphina drew in her breath.

Suddenly she felt the words were there and she could say them to him.

"What is it?" he asked.

Then before she could answer a servant stood in the door-way.

"Excuse me, Sahib," he said, "but a messenger has arrived with two cables."

"Cables? At this hour of night?" Kelvin Ward exclaimed.

"We have no telegraph line," the servant explained, "and the messenger knew that the cables were urgent."

He handed them to Kelvin as he spoke, who took them from the round tray on which they were presented.

He sat up in his chair and opened the first one, which was addressed to Major Kelvin Ward.

He read it through. Then as the servant withdrew Seraphina said, a nervous note in her voice:

"What is it? What has happened?"

She knew without being told that her husband was tense.

There was something in the manner in which he was holding the piece of paper between his fingers which frightened her.

In answer he read aloud:

"Deeply regret to inform you that His Grace the Duke of Uxbridge died this morning of

an unexpected heart-attack. Funeral will
take place Friday.

> Meredith, Mayhew and Leach."

"Your Uncle is dead!" Seraphina exclaimed
unnecessarily.

Kelvin did not answer.

Instead he picked up the other cable and saw
it was addressed to His Grace, the Duke of
Uxbridge.

As he opened it he realised it had been sent
two days after the first one.

It had either been delayed in transit to Bombay or else had been held up at Chitorgarh until
they had a messenger they could send to Udaipur.

He read the message to himself and then again
in a voice curiously devoid of emotion he read
aloud:

We beg to inform Your Grace that the Estate of the late Duke has been valued at approximately three million pounds. We are
administering both households and properties until we receive Your Grace's instructions.

> Meredith, Mayhew and Leach."

As Kelvin finished reading the telegram he
rose to his feet.

"At last!" he exclaimed. "I am free of your
damned money!"

Seraphina stood very still.

Then before she could speak, before she could
even move, the servant came back into the room
carrying a blotter, inkwell and white quill pen.

"I thought the Sahib might wish to send a return cable," he said respectfully. "The messenger is
waiting."

He placed the blotter on the table in front of
Kelvin, who looked at it for a moment and sat
down.

"Yes, tell the man to wait," he said and picked up the pen.

He wrote out a cable to the Solicitors and as he read it through a figure appeared in the doorway.

"Forgive my intrusion," the Purdhan said, "but His Highness, having heard the news, has asked me to bring you first his deepest condolences on your esteemed Uncle's death and secondly His Highness's best wishes for the distinguished position you now hold."

Kelvin was not surprised that already the Maharana knew the contents of the cables.

Everything was known in India and the messenger would not have travelled without being aware of the message he carried.

He would also have been unable to keep the information to himself once he arrived at Udaipur.

"Thank you," Kelvin said.

"I hope this does not mean that you will leave us?"

"I see no reason to do so," Kelvin Ward replied. "It will take us a month to get home to England from here and whether we stay in India a few more days or weeks before starting on the return journey is really of little consequence."

He picked up the cable he had written and handed it to the waiting servant.

"Ask the messenger to convey this to Chitorgarh as soon as possible," he said, "and there are others I would wish to send in the morning."

"There will be no difficulty about that," the Purdhan said as the servant left the room.

"My wife and I have been made so welcome here by His Highness and also by you, Your Excellency," Kelvin said, "that it would be foolish of us to hurry away, or indeed to rush back to England."

"I am indeed glad of that," the Purdhan smiled.

"There are Attorneys who can cope with everything in my absence."

Kelvin could not prevent a note of satisfaction creeping into his voice.

It seemed unbelievable after all his Uncle had said—after his parsimonious cheese-parings, his moans of poverty, the needless economies at the expense of his relatives—that he should have died a very wealthy man.

Already Kelvin found himself thinking of how he could improve the properties, increase the wages of the servants, raise the pensions of those who had retired and of the part he himself could now play in politics.

Yet even as he thought of it he knew he had no desire at present to return to England.

His heart was in India—it always had been so, and he had a feeling that for Seraphina too it already meant home.

Courtesy in the East cannot be hurried and the Purdhan sat down obviously anxious to discuss Kelvin's new position and to learn details of his Estates.

It was nearly an hour before Kelvin could be rid of him but at last he bowed himself out and Kelvin again expressed his appreciation of the Maharana's kindness and his gratitude for both His Highness's condolences and congratulations.

When the Purdhan had gone Kelvin walked back into the Salon and picked up the cables.

Two cables! Two messages at 4/9d a word which had changed his whole future!

It was then that he thought of Seraphina and knew that he must talk to her.

It had been infuriating to have to discuss his private affairs first with a stranger when he would rather have been talking of them with her.

He had seen her slip away as the Purdhan arrived and thought that she had no desire to be embroiled in the flowery Eastern exchange of pleasantries which were correct for such an occasion as this.

Kelvin walked from the Salon and up the marble stairs to the balcony.

Their rooms joined each other and he knew that to their hosts it would seem incredible for them not to spend the night in each other's arms.

There was no light under Seraphina's door and Kelvin having raised his hand to knock lowered it again.

Very gently he turned the handle.

There was just enough light coming from the windows for him to see the outline of Seraphina's bed with her head against the pillows.

She did not speak and he thought she must be asleep.

He listened. Then he said in a very low whisper:

"Seraphina!"

She did not answer and after a moment he went from the room, closing the door behind him.

For a moment after he had gone Seraphina lay very still. Then she turned over and buried her face in the pillows.

She knew now that everything for which she longed was hopeless.

Kelvin had spoken the truth.

It had come spontaneously from his lips and he had not tried to soften or express it so as not to hurt her.

For her there was no "*passion springing in his heart.*"

She was of no further use to him.

Seraphina did not cry. She only knew the agony she was feeling was past tears, past anything, but a misery so dark, so utterly hopeless it was like being in hell.

"If only I could . . . die!" she whispered. "If only I was . . . dead!"

Chapter Eight

Kelvin came down to breakfast.

The sunshine was almost blinding on the white marble and the purple bougainvillaea and yellow jasmine glowed like jewels against the mosaics.

He had awakened very early to lie thinking of all the things he wanted to do in the future, and he knew that one ambition at least would come true.

The evening they had dined with the Governor in Bombay when the ladies had left the verandah, he had asked Kelvin to move up the table to sit beside him.

The other guests were talking amongst themselves and the Governor had said in a low voice:

"There is something I want to tell you."

"What is it, Sir?" Kelvin asked.

"I am going home in July because I have to have an operation."

"I am very sorry to hear that!" Kelvin exclaimed.

"I am telling you this in confidence," the Governor went on, "because I have always been fond of you and because my early retirement will I hope affect you."

"Affect me?" Kelvin questioned in surprise.

"Next week," the Governor replied, "I will be seeing the Viceroy and I am going to suggest that both he and I put forward your name as the next Governor of Bombay."

Kelvin did not speak for a moment. Then he said quietly:

"I doubt if the Prime Minister will accept such a recommendation."

"That remains to be seen," the Governor replied. "At the same time I am told they are anxious in England to make Governorships not just a comfortable retirement for aged Generals but to appoint younger men who have a knowledge of the country."

"That could certainly be an improvement," Kelvin Ward agreed.

"I know of no-one who could fill such a position better than you," the Governor went on, "and while it would have been impossible for you in the past, obviously circumstances have now changed."

Kelvin was aware that the Governor was referring tactfully to the alteration in his financial position arising from his marriage.

"Naturally if your Uncle were dead," he continued, "the situation would be even easier, if you were then prepared to accept such a position."

He smiled.

"It is hard work! That is if you do the job properly!"

"I am aware of that!" Kelvin said. "You must know, Sir, there is nothing I should enjoy more."

"There are few young men in India," the Governor said, "who have your knowledge of the country and its people, and perhaps I should add your affection for them."

Kelvin did not need to tell the Governor, whom he had known for many years, how deeply involved his affections were for India and its peoples.

"It is unnecessary for me to say," the Governor went on, "that this conversation must not be repeated to anyone. But I shall be very surprised if in a month or so you do not hear from the Prime Minister!"

"I shall hope very much you are right, Sir," Kelvin replied.

It might however have been difficult for the Prime Minister to appoint him however good his qualifications, had his social position not been assured.

There were few if any Dukes who were agreeable to serve five years in India, and Kelvin knew the chance of his becoming Governor of Bombay was now almost an odds-on certainty.

He had on waking made a decision which was an entirely personal one.

It was that he would ask Sir Anthony Fanshawe to look after the Uxbridge Estates.

'It will give Anthony something to do,' he told himself, 'and he is well qualified for the job.'

It would under the circumstances be easy to pay Anthony for such services without his being too proud to accept money from a friend.

What was more, with Anthony in charge there was no reason for him to return to England until he was ready to do so.

He had no wish to take Seraphina back so soon after they had arrived, and if he was honest with himself he had no desire to encounter Sir Erasmus again.

He had a feeling that Seraphina was very much happier because she was not over-shadowed by her father's domination and over-powering personality, and from his own point of view the greater the distance between his father-in-law and himself, the better.

"We will stay in India," Kelvin Ward decided,

"at least for the next few months, and after that . . ."

There was a faint smile on his lips as he thought of the future.

He would not, he thought, keep Seraphina in the heat of Bombay. They could go North and stay either at Simla or visit Kashmir.

The foothills of the Himalayas would be cool and in a month or so would be brilliant with flowers as beautiful and fragrant as Seraphina herself.

It seemed to Kelvin as he looked out over the lake at the beauty of the Palaces, pale gold in the morning sunlight, that a while new vista was opening out in front of him.

At last all the things he really wanted in life were coming true!

He would be able to advise, inspire and command, and that after all was what he had been trained to do in the long years he had served in the Army.

Now he would reap the benefit of having struggled to learn so many of the different languages of India so that he could talk to the people.

"You are wasting your time, Ward," many of his brother Officers said to him when he had preferred to go off camping in the country rather than play polo.

They would laugh at him when he stayed up late at night studying Sanskrit rather than sit drinking in the Mess.

Kelvin told himself that at last all the knowledge he had accumulated would be put to its proper use.

There were so many things he could do once he was in the position to implement his ideas—a closer co-operation with Indian Government authorities, Clubs where Indians as well as Europeans would be welcome, more social integration.

Seraphina would be an immeasurable help

with the social side. He had already seen how friendly and at ease she was with Indian women.

There was a great deal to do! There would be of course opposition to such revolutionary ideas.

But at least he would have the opportunity.

"The gods are kind," he murmured.

Then turning from the window he walked towards the breakfast-table.

He saw that it had only been laid for one and as he sat down he asked the servant:

"Is the Memsahib having breakfast in her room?"

"The Memsahib has left, Sahib."

"Left?" Kelvin asked.

He tried to remember if Seraphina had told him last night that there was something special arranged for this morning.

He decided the man had misunderstood him.

"I asked," he said slowly, "if the Memsahib is having breakfast in her bed-room?"

"No, Sahib."

Kelvin waited and the servant added:

"The Memsahib left very early soon after dawn."

Kelvin rose from the table.

For a moment he felt he could not understand what the man was trying to say to him. Then without asking any further questions, he walked across the sun-lit court-yard and up the marble stairs to the balcony.

He reached Seraphina's room, knocked and opened the door at the same time.

The room was empty!

The bed-clothes were thrown back, but a wardrobe door was open and Kelvin could see some gowns hanging within it.

He felt a sudden fear inside himself subside.

She must have gone to see the Rajmata, he thought, and wondered why she had not informed him of the arrangement.

Then he saw a letter lying on the dressing-table.

He knew before he crossed the room that it would be addressed to him. He took it up and was afraid to open it.

Very slowly he drew out a sheet of writing-paper from the envelope and read:

> Now that you have everything you want, I am going back to Papa. Please do not try to stop me. I understand what you feel and I can only thank you for being so kind and patient with me.
>
> Seraphina

Kelvin felt as if the words danced in front of his eyes and he could not understand them. Then he raised his head to look round the room he had not entered since they had been at the Lake Palace.

White and cool, it was a very beautiful and fitting background for Seraphina.

There was also the faint, sweet fragrance of her scent which he noticed whenever she was near him.

He squared his chin and walked from the room.

He sent for his own servant Jahan.

"Why did you not inform me when the Memsahib left early this morning?" he asked.

"The Memsahib most insistent we should not wake you, Sahib."

"Who went with her?"

"Only Amar."

"Did Amar say where they were going?"

"No, Sahib."

"I am leaving now and you are coming with me!" Kelvin said. "We travel on horse-back. Bring things for the night."

"Yes, Sahib. We will be coming back?"

"We will be coming back!" Kelvin repeated and his voice was firm.

Half an hour later they left the Palace, Kelvin riding one of the horses that had been given to him as a present by the Maharana.

It was a magnificent animal with a touch of Arab in it. When he reached the stables he had asked for another horse for his servant.

"There is only one other horse as good as the one you will be riding, Sahib," he was told, "and that is already yours."

The horses had been saddled and bridled with ordinary harnessing, not the silver and gold accoutrements which had been part of the present from the Maharana.

Jahan tied a rolled blanket onto the back of his saddle and they set off, moving from the moment they left the Palace at a speed which Kelvin intended to maintain during the long ride ahead.

He knew that he would have to ride swiftly if he was to prevent Seraphina reaching Bombay before him and leaving for England on the first available ship.

Once she had done that it might be weeks before he could catch up with her. It was therefore absolutely essential that he should reach her before she arrived at Chitorgarh.

He had learnt quite easily what was her destination and that she was travelling in a tonga—a small, very light Indian cart with large wheels and drawn by one horse.

She would move with speed, and having left before four-thirty in the morning she would by this time be many miles ahead of him.

Kelvin was too experienced a horseman to push his mount however spirited. He and Jahan held their horses in check until they settled into a swift, even pace which was not too exhausting either for horses or riders.

Fortunately once they had left Udaipur the road to Chitorgarh was mostly over a flat plain and the ground was soft.

Kelvin found himself going over and over in his mind everything that had happened since he'd married.

He blamed himself entirely for what had happened now.

He should have known that Seraphina would interpret what he had said when he read the cables in a way he had not meant, and he knew that he should have followed her the moment she left the room.

Failing that he should have awakened her, if indeed she had really been asleep when after the Purdhan had left he had gone to her room.

'I have been a fool!' Kelvin told himself honestly.

Now his only excuse could be that while he was vastly experienced with sophisticated women he had never before met anyone like Seraphina.

Always women had been attracted to him, and almost before his own desire for them was aroused they had shown their willingness to fall into his arms, to give him whatever he asked.

From the very beginning Seraphina had reminded him of a fawn that he had tried to tame when he was a small boy.

At first it had run away in fear whenever he approached; then an old game-keeper who had some Gypsy in his blood had explained that first the fawn must grow used to him and accept him as nothing strange or unusual.

He could remember sitting for hours under a tree in the Park at home not moving, just watching the fawn come nearer and nearer to him until it would be almost within reach.

Then one hasty movement, even a noisy breath, would frighten it and it would speed away and he would have to start all over again.

It had taken him months but finally the fawn had eaten out of his hand and would come to him when he called it.

He remembered how sensitive it had seemed with its huge eyes and slender legs. It also had a grace which he inevitably compared with Seraphina.

He had never before known a woman could be so graceful, just as he had never before known a woman who looked at him in fear, or who later had been so responsive to his every mood.

He had known that she watched him from under her eye-lashes apprehensively when he came into the room in case he was angry.

She would look at him too for approval not only of her appearance, but when she said something to other people which she hoped was right.

She was such a child in so many ways, and yet he had never known a woman who thought so deeply or who had so many original ideas.

He remembered now how they had talked on the ship about religion, philosophy and psychology.

He had never expected any woman to think such subjects important, let alone to have any knowledge of them.

And her sensitive understanding of humanity had astounded him. She looked always for a deeper meaning, for the motive behind the action, the world behind the world.

She was such an extraordinary mixture—half child, half woman—and so incredibly, unbelievably innocent.

'And surely,' Kelvin asked himself as he rode along, 'this, if they had the choice, is what all men would desire?'

He thought of the Maharanee and knew that in many ways Seraphina resembled the Indian woman, in her femininity, her compassion and sweetness.

The manner in which Seraphina was so pliable and ready to learn made her very unlike the average English girl who was sure of herself, positive in her opinions, quite certain she was God's gift to the world!

Now he knew Seraphina was unhappy—suffering because of his stupidity.

"I must get to her!"

Without meaning to Kelvin pressed his mount a little harder.

They stopped at midday to water the horses and give them a short rest.

Jahan would have bought food in a village through which they had passed but Kelvin required nothing except a cold drink.

He had eaten no breakfast but he was not hungry.

He was only possessed by an urgency within himself which made him impervious to hunger.

They rode on even through the heat of the day and then as the horses began to tire, Kelvin realised that soon it would be dark. There was an anxiety in his expression which made his servant look at him apprehensively.

They made enquiries at the villages through which they passed and at all of them they learnt that a tonga containing a Memsahib was still ahead of them.

Then on the outskirts of a small town they saw a dak-bungalow.

All over India there were dak-bungalows erected for European travellers who must stay the night on their journey.

Sometimes they were quite large and impressive, but this was only a very small building, and at a glance Kelvin knew that it contained two bedrooms and a communal Dining-Room.

Behind there would be a hut for the *Khansamah*, or keeper, and stabling for horses.

The bungalow stood in a garden bright with flowers.

"We shall have to stay here," Kelvin said to his servant.

He could not imagine as they turned in at the gate where Seraphina could be staying.

Surely Amar would have the sense to find her a dak-bungalow?

Kelvin had called at the Palaces where they had stayed on their journey to Udaipur. He had hoped that Seraphina might have returned there, yet at the same time he had known it was unlikely.

There would have been need of explanations as to why she was travelling alone.

There was also the chance that their previous hosts would have thought it so extraordinary that they would have been reluctant to let her go on with her journey.

'She cannot be so very far ahead,' Kelvin told himself as he rode behind the dak-bungalow to where he knew the stables would be.

As he reached them he saw a tonga!

It was horseless, its shafts on the ground and as Kelvin dismounted he saw Amar looking out at him from the stable.

"Amar!" he called. "Where is the Memsahib?"

"She has retired to bed, Sahib, but I'm glad you have come!"

Kelvin drew a deep breath.

For the moment there was no more urgency.

He had found her!

"The Memsahib is all right?" he asked.

"A little tired, Sahib. We have come a long way."

"You have indeed!"

"We changed horses," Amar explained. "We had to pay quite a number of rupees, but the Memsahib said it did not matter."

"No, it did not matter!" Kelvin repeated and he walked towards the dak-bungalow.

The *Khansamah* ceremoniously ushered him into the small narrow bed-room. It contained only a charpoy—an Indian bed, a table and a chair.

Travellers in India carried everything else they required with them.

"There is a Memsahib in the other room," the *Khansamah* explained unnecessarily.

"Yes, I know," Kelvin answered.

Jahan came in with the blanket which had been attached to his saddle.

He unrolled it. Inside was a clean shirt and other garments besides a box of razors and washing requisites.

For the first time since he had set out from the Palace Kelvin found he was hungry.

He also realised that he was covered in a fine dust which had been thrown up by the horses' hooves on the dry road.

"I will wash!" he said abruptly.

There was a washing-place next to his bedroom where there were buckets of water standing beside a sluice.

He was cool and hungry when he came back into the bed-room wrapped only in a towel to find that Jahan had brought with them the long blue robe which Sir Anthony had made him buy in St. James's.

He put it on and Jahan served him with food and a bottle of Indian beer which had been kept cold in the well.

Kelvin ate although he had no idea what the food tasted like.

When Jahan had left him and he was alone he stood indecisively for some moments thinking of what he should do.

Then he told himself that last night when Seraphina had been asleep he had gone away and it had been a mistake.

If she learnt he was here she might run away from him again, and that he was determined to prevent.

Quietly he walked across the Dining-Room which lay between the two bed-rooms.

It was unlit and he saw there was a faint shaft of light beneath Seraphina's door.

He hoped she would still be awake. He was half-afraid that he would frighten her if she awoke suddenly to find him there.

Very gently and without knocking he opened the door.

One candle flickered on a table by the bed which was covered with a mosquito net.

Kneeling on the ground beside it was Seraphina.

She had not heard the door open and Kelvin stood watching her while she was unaware of his presence.

She was praying and her hands covered her face.

Then after a few seconds as if instinctively she knew she was being watched she turned her head towards him and he saw the tears were running down her cheeks.

For a moment she did not speak or move but only looked at him, her eyes seeming to fill her small face.

"Who are you praying for, Seraphina?" Kelvin asked in his deep voice.

"For . . . you," she answered as if she spoke without thinking.

"And are the tears for me too?" he asked.

Nervously she rose to her feet.

She looked like a child who had been caught out in an act of truancy and was waiting to be reprimanded.

But behind her the candle silhouetted her body beneath the fine lawn of her night-gown.

Slender though she was it was not a child's body he saw.

"Get into bed, Seraphina," Kelvin said quietly. "I want to talk to you."

She obeyed him, lifting the folds of the

mosquito netting from the ground and disappearing inside it.

Kelvin blew out the candle and opened the window.

While he had been in the bungalow night had come and the sky had filled with stars.

The moon had also risen and it filled the small, bare room with silver rays so bright, so brilliant that when he raised the mosquito netting Kelvin could see Seraphina's face as clearly as if it were day.

There was only one pillow behind her tonight and one sheet to cover her.

She still looked frail and fairy-like and he thought under the shadowy mist of the mosquito netting she might have been the figment of a dream.

He sat down on the side of the bed. There was no fear in her expression but her eyes, with her lashes wet from her tears, were worried and apprehensive.

"I thought I should never catch up with you," he said.

"I told you . . . not to follow . . . me."

"I had to."

"W-why?"

"For one reason, because what you said to me in your letter was untrue."

"Untrue?" she asked questioningly.

"You said I had everything I wanted in life."

"But you have . . . your Uncle is . . . dead and you are . . . rich!"

It was difficult to say the last word.

"I still want something else," Kelvin said. "Something far more important than either of those things."

"What is . . . that?"

"You!"

He saw her quiver but she did not speak.

"I want to tell you something, Seraphina, something I should have told you before now."

"What is . . . it?"

"When I came to your room the night we were married, I expected to find a big, bossy woman, rather like your father, waiting for me."

He smiled.

"You know what I discovered: someone very small and frightened."

There was a note in his voice which made her drop her eyes.

"I tried to be kind and understanding," he went on. "I told myself that you needed to be helped and protected. But I also fell in love with you."

"It . . . is not . . . true!"

Seraphina could hardly breathe the words.

"It is true!" he answered, "and I acknowledged to myself what had happened when you clung to me during the storm at sea. Then when we talked together aboard ship, I found I not only had to protect you from being frightened but to polish up my brains to keep up with yours!"

Seraphina made a little movement as if of protest.

"Every day of that voyage I fell more in love with you," he went on. "The one who was afraid was not you, Seraphina. It was I! I was desperately afraid of driving you away from me by destroying the trust I believed you were beginning to give me."

She looked up at him for a moment and he saw a sudden light in her eyes as if a thousand candles had been lit inside her.

"I knew," he went on, "when I saw you sitting on the deck in your pink gown holding that injured Indian child tenderly in your arms that you were everything that a man could long for and desire."

He saw Seraphina's whole body tremble and knew it was not with fear.

Then he said:

"When you saved the little Prince and I saw you coming towards me through a wall of fire, I realised that if I lost you I would have lost everything that mattered to me in life."

There was a note in his voice that made Seraphina feel as if she vibrated to some strange and enchanted music.

"I should have told you all these things," Kelvin said, "but I was not only afraid of your reaction, but there was also a barrier between us."

"My . . . money!" Seraphina murmured.

"Yes, your money!" he answered. "I resented it and hated it because you are so sensitive and so absurdly vulnerable, my darling, that you might have thought I was being affectionate to you merely in return for it."

He sighed before he went on:

"How, I asked myself, could I make love to you if it even so much as crossed your mind it might be repayment for what I had gained by our marriage?"

He paused, then added:

"That is why last night when the cables came, my first reaction was one of sheer relief that the absurb barrier which existed between us had gone!"

Seraphina's eyes were wide and without moving he said very softly:

"I love you, my precious! I love you more than I believed it possible to love any woman, and now there is nothing to stop me from telling you so!"

She did not speak and after a moment he said:

"I will be very gentle with you, Seraphina. I will not touch you until you ask me to, but will you please stay with me? I want you desperately!"

It was impossible for Seraphina to answer, the whole world golden and blinding seemed to be whirling round her.

At last she faltered:

"I . . . will . . . s-stay."

"My precious, my poor frightened little love—
we will be happy, I swear it! But be kind to me,
Seraphina!"

"Kind?"

"Darling, you do not understand how hard it
is for me to keep away from you, not to kiss you,
not to make you mine."

Kelvin paused, then with his voice deepening
he went on:

"Every night on the ship I would think of you
so near to me but with your door shut, and I could
not sleep. I wanted you, my lovely one. I wanted
you agonizingly."

He heard Seraphina draw in her breath.

"And the other night," he went on, "when I
carried you to bed it was a torture I can never describe to let you go."

His voice was passionate as he continued:

"I kissed your hand because I could not help
myself but I wanted to kiss your lips, your hair,
your eyes . . . !"

He checked himself to sav more quietly:

"One day, when you will let me, I will kiss you
from the top of your clever little head to your ridic-
ulously small feet and then you will understand."

Seraphina's hands went up to her breasts as if
to still the tumult in them.

"I worship you!" Kelvin said softly, "but I
also desire you with every nerve in my body. I did
not know a woman could be so utterly and completely desirable."

Seraphina saw the fire in his eyes and then
when she would have spoken he said as if he spoke
to himself:

"But I must not frighten you."

In another tone he asked:

"Will you tell me what you were going to say
to me last night before that servant interrupted us?
I feel somehow it was important."

She made a convulsive little movement as if she would reach out to him, but she did not speak.

"Tell me, Seraphina."

Then, as he waited, in a voice so low he could hardly hear it she said:

"Could . . . could you . . . come very close . . . really close so that . . . I can . . . tell you?"

At first Kelvin thought he had not understood! Then his robe fell to the ground, he slipped under the sheet and very gently, almost as if he took a flower into his arms, he drew her to him.

"Please tell me, my darling one," he pleaded.

He could feel her quivering against him as with her head on his shoulder she raised her face to his.

"I . . . I . . . was going to . . . tell you," she whispered, "that I am . . . no longer afraid and I want . . . to be your . . . wife . . . your real . . . wife!"

Kelvin held her so tightly against him that she could hardly breathe. Then his lips sought hers.

It was a kiss as soft and delicate as a butterfly hovering above a blossom, and yet Seraphina felt that flicker of fire which she had felt before waken within her.

It was an ecstasy and a wonder that she had never known, something beyond words, so wonderful, so marvellous that instinctively she pressed herself closer, feeling his body hard against the softness of hers.

He raised his head and said in a voice that was curiously unsteady:

"My beautiful darling, I did not mean to make love to you for the first time in anything as un-romantic as a dak-bungalow!"

"It is an . . . enchanted Palace!"

"Do you mean that?" he asked. "And am I perhaps after all your Prince Charming?"

"You are so . . . so much more," she answered.

"To me you are the world . . . the sky . . . the god of love . . . Krishna!"

"My precious! My sweet! How can you say such things to me?" Kelvin asked.

Then once again he was kissing her and this time his lips were gentle but possessive, tender but demanding.

They took possession of her and she surrendered herself to the fire he aroused in her, fire so rapturous, so divine she was no longer herself but a part of him.

"I . . . love you . . . I love y-you!"

She could hardly breathe the words.

"I adore you—my perfect little wife."

Then there was only the magic of the moonlight and the soft, sweet cry of love.

SPECIAL OFFER: If you enjoyed this book and would like to have our catalog of over 1,400 other Bantam titles, just send your name and address and 25¢ (to help defray postage and handling costs) to: Catalog Department, Bantam Books, Inc., 414 East Golf Rd., Des Plaines, Ill. 60016.